DALTON HIGHWAY

FREDDIE ÅHLIN

SHARP ARROW
PUBLISHING

ISBN: 978-91-519-5470-7 (Paperback)
       978-91-519-5529-2 (Hardback)
       978-91-519-5471-4 (Ebook)

Any references to historical events, real people, or real places are used fictitiously. Names, characters, and places are products of the author's imagination.

First printing edition 2020.

Sharp Arrow Publishing

Cover design artist: Milan Jovanovic
Interior Design by FormattedBooks.com

This book is dedicated to my sons,
who inspire me to endless imagination.
-Freddie Åhlin

PART
ONE

CHAPTER

1

THERE IS A MOMENT in every man's life when his gaze reveals how the world he once took for granted no longer offers the same kind of security and hope it once did. For Tom Richards, that realization came at the age of forty-five, on a Friday morning in September, when he sat at the kitchen table and glanced out the window overlooking his and his wife's farm, located on the edge of Fairbanks, Alaska. The window reflected how his unshaven, sunken face faded into deep shadows, while his well-worn jeans and thick, flannel shirt hung on his wiry frame.

Overhead, an army of gloomy clouds caused shadows to dance over swaying treetops, while a dense fog crept forward along the main road, shifting both the tree roots and grass from their original shape. Wind tore through the bushes with a hollow shriek and made the branches shiver, while a bird chirped somewhere to the north.

Summer had faded, and it wouldn't be long before winter would come to Alaska.

The local radio station, 102.5 KIAK FM, had earlier that morning announced a heavy storm threatened the outskirts of Fairbanks. But the truth was it had already arrived. It had been sneaking around out there the whole night, howling with all its might each time Tom tried to close his eyes. The storm had forced him out of bed sometime in the early hours, and he had walked down to the kitchen, boiled some coffee, and then stared out at the main road, until he found himself bouncing his right knee like a sewing machine needle. He had a long weekend ahead out there. Bad weather was the last thing he needed.

In a couple of minutes, he would take his pickup to work a few miles up the road. From there, he would make the longest journey of his trucking career. He would deliver boxes of tools to an oil field at the farthest spot on Dalton Highway, a 414-mile isolated stretch that went from northern Fairbanks to a small town located near the Arctic Ocean called Deadhorse, in Prudhoe Bay. Including only three small towns along the way, with nothing more than total seclusion the last 238 miles, it would take him a whole day to get there. Not being able to unload until daylight, he'd be forced to spend Friday night in his truck, on a cold, dark oil field, in the middle of nowhere, listening to the overwhelming sounds of the violent storms and the eternal sea beyond. But he did what he had to do. This was a once-in-a-lifetime opportunity. He wasn't young anymore, and life wasn't getting any easier.

He sighed.

When a sudden movement appeared at the edge of his vision, Tom twitched, sure if he turned around, something horrific from the fog— *something* that didn't belong to the ordinary world—would be behind him. But when the voice of his wife asked him if he couldn't sleep, the fear drained away. Margaret stood in the doorway with her silvery, silk robe wrapped around her curved body, as her golden hair fell along her bony shoulders. After fifteen years, she was still as beautiful as she was curious, and sometimes Tom wondered why she hadn't left him for someone better. In that moment, he wanted to embrace her and never let go, but he couldn't move a finger.

"Did the storm wake you up?" she wondered, and twisted the gold ring on her finger. It was the ring Tom had given her when things were different, when their future together seemed bright. "I don't want you to drive if you haven't slept any."

Tom clenched his jaw. "You know how much we need the money, Maggie."

"What if you fall asleep while driving?"

He shrugged. "I'm taking Presley with me. He'll keep me company."

The dog heard his name and shoved past Margaret. He wagged his tail like a Ferris wheel and looked up at Tom. He was a five-year-old German Shepherd, who still had the mind of a puppy, but also loved to sleep like he was double his age. They had named him after the King of Rock.

"Right, buddy?" Tom scratched behind the dog's ear. "You're gonna keep me good company, right? Good boy."

Presley pressed himself against Tom's legs with a whine and demanded attention.

Margaret glanced out the window. "This storm is getting worse."

"Listen," Tom said and sighed, "I *have* to go."

Margaret walked to the sink with a secretive, dark sigh. "So we can pay this one?" She picked up a letter next to the dirty stove. "And this? And *this?*" She grabbed a stack of bills in her hands, and her voice broke. "You know I can call my mother, and—"

"No!" Tom said and almost knocked his coffee cup off the table. "I will not let you call her. She has nothing to do with this. She—"

"But, Tom—"

"I said, no!" He pulled his hand through his greasy hair and scratched his itching stubble with a deep sigh. Something else he needed to do, but he'd take a shower and shave when he got home, not enough time now.

Margaret turned to the window and dropped the bills on the floor.

Tom sighed.

"Do you think they will take it this time?" Margaret asked in a low voice. "Do you think we'll lose our house?"

Tom looked past her for a second when the kitchen window rattled. Then he said, "Do you really think I'm going to let them do that?"

A few drops of rain pressed themselves against the glass, as if they were the audience for the other storm, the one brewing inside the house.

"I need to go to the bathroom," Margaret sobbed.

Tom followed her presence as she walked out from the kitchen. He sighed. Why did everything lead to a fight nowadays? Didn't she get that he wanted the best for *her?* He did what he could. Wasn't it enough?

What are you waiting for? Apologize, you moron!

Tom took a deep breath and got up from the chair, bringing the coffee cup with him. He didn't need a fight on his conscience when he left. "Hey, Maggie," he said on his way towards the bathroom. "I don't want to discuss this now. I don't want to fight before leaving. I *will* fix this. I just don't—"

But something made him still outside the bathroom. It was a low cry coming from inside. The door was ajar.

Tom bent closer.

"But he doesn't want to," Margaret whispered. "I know, mom, but he won't listen. He isn't himself anymore. I don't know what to do anyway. No he doesn't wanna take his medicines anymore—"

Tom clenched his jaw and stumbled back down the hall.

"Tom?" Margaret said from the bathroom. "Are you out there?"

He ignored her and walked back to the kitchen. He stepped over the bills and slammed the coffee cup on the counter. "Come on, Presley!"

When they walked out to the hall, Margaret came out of the bathroom. "Are you leaving already?"

Tom glared at her and said nothing.

"What's wrong, Tom?"

"Don't you think I know what you did?" he sneered at her. "Do you really think I'm that *stupid* I don't even get what the hell you're doing?"

Margaret lost her words. A few tears raged on each side of her cheeks.

"Don't you get I'm doing all this for you!?" he continued. "I would never let them take this house from us! I work my ass off, and for what? So you can call your mother and ask for more money?"

"What I need is *this* house," Margaret said. "A place that—"

"I know!" he interrupted her. "I fucking *know!* And I *will* fix it. Do you hear me?"

"Why can't you two just forget the past?" Margaret sobbed.

"Forget it?" Tom laughed a short one. "She had her chance, Margaret! And she screwed it!" He put on a sun-bleached cap and a yellow raincoat that made him look more like a typical road worker than an old trucker. If he had learned anything from years of driving on the road, it was that clothes could save you when nothing else could. He bent down and put on his black leather boots one by one. "What more do you want me to do?"

"Forgive her."

"Forgive *her*?"

"Don't be ridiculous, Tom." Margaret shook her head. "Why don't you give it a chance?"

Tom pulled the collar over Presley's head, and the round silvery name tag clinked against the chain of the leash. "Do you remember what she said at Thanksgiving a few years ago in front of everybody?"

Margaret sighed. "I remember."

Tom pressed his lips together to keep from saying anything. He grabbed the backpack he had packed the day before. He'd tossed in a few bottles of water, a bag of dog food, two bags of Jack Link's beef jerky, a few Hershey's bars, a bag of salted, mixed nuts, and some dried fruits. He had also packed a homemade map of Dalton Highway that he, after some time, had managed to get out of the cursed printer upstairs. The rest of the necessities were already in the truck, company issued.

"But things *have* changed, Tom. It was a long time ago."

Tom smiled. "How? How have things changed? Has your mother lost her tongue? I'm sure she—"

"Stop it!"

Presley's ears went flat against his head, and his eyes got wide.

"You're scaring Presley," Tom said in a low voice. "I don't like when you scare him."

Margaret placed her hands against her face and took a deep breath. "All I'm asking for is you to respect that she's my mother. To see you two in the same room. Is it too much to ask for, to let her help us?"

"We both know your mother *hates* me." Tom bared his teeth. "If she could, she would throw me to hungry dogs, bury me alive, and—"

"That's not true!" Tears ran down her cheeks.

"You know it's true!" Tom patted his raincoat pocket violently to check for the keys. Both the pickup keys and the truck keys were there. His wallet was in another pocket. He had to bring it because of the poor signals out there, where no credit card would work. "And the worst part, Maggie, do you know what that is?" He didn't let her answer. "The worst part is that you *let* her. Yes, *you* let her treat me like I was a bag of garbage!" Tom threw the backpack on his shoulder and opened the front door. It flew open, and he had to hang on to it for a few seconds until the wind relaxed. The air outside had a damp thickness, as if he had opened the door into an invisible field of steam.

"Come on, buddy!"

Presley went out, tail between his legs to protest the storm.

Margaret came close behind. "Please, Tom—"

Tom turned around, and the wind almost snatched his cap away. "I don't wanna hear anymore! I'm tired of all of this!"

A growling noise sounded from above, like a massive wolf waiting to attack, and Presley strained at the leash. Tom was pulled along, away from the door. "Hey, take it easy!" he shouted. "You won't even let me have a damn smoke, will you?"

He didn't; the dog pushed forward across the courtyard, eager to get inside the pickup.

After Presley jumped in the pickup, Tom sighed and turned again. Margaret stood by the front door with her robe flicking in the wind. In that moment, Tom could have walked up to her and apologized, but he didn't. Instead, he shook his head, got in the pickup, and left.

CHAPTER

2

WHEN TOM AND PRESLEY arrived at the company's parking lot, where the already filled truck was ready for transport, the clouds had darkened, and the wind thundered more with every second that passed. The changeover from the pickup to the truck went quick, and Presley shook when they got inside the cab.

Tom threw the backpack on the floor below Presley, and the seat gnawed at him as he settled in. Even though the wind pushed through the open door and made him shiver, he had to leave it ajar for another few minutes to do a control check. It wasn't something he liked to do, but it was something he *had* to do.

"What do you think, buddy?" Tom said with a sigh. "You think we'll get out of here today?" He inserted the driver card into the digital tachograph. It kept track of the speed, driving time, and even his breaks, all without him doing anything. "Let's find out."

To control check, he pushed down the brake and tried to listen through the open door to detect any sort of air leakage. The rule was to listen for three minutes, but sometimes he cheated.

He pumped out air so the blocking valve could pop out. When it did, it let out a whoosh, the same kind of noise an iron gives when the steam setting is engaged. He turned the ignition, and the motor started to chew. "Come on you piece of shit," Tom whispered. "Start!"

Nothing happened.

He turned the ignition once more, and this time, the truck started to vibrate.

Tom smiled. "There we go."

Presley looked at Tom, his small, dark eyes distressed, as a dreadful twist dug out from his throat.

"You want to leave, don't you?"

Presley sat up, and his tongue fell out of his mouth; his ears perked straight up.

Tom listened. It didn't take long before the tachometer beeped. Good. One less thing to worry about.

Above them, the sky turned darker, and in the distance, the sound of a fire truck whined.

As Tom waited for the air pressure to rise, he turned the heat on full. The air broke out over the panel by the front window. He let the windshield wipers pull right, left, right, and sprayed the windshield fluid. No problem. He honked the horn, and Presley winced, as if he were about to take off. The dog had never liked those wailing sounds. Sometimes he'd howl along with them, singing some kind of melody or screaming out a painful rhythm. But not this time. This time he was all quiet, like he knew what would happen in the next few hours.

When the air pressure was ready, Tom shifted gears to see if the shut-off valve worked and released the parking brake to make everything fall in order. "It seems like we're getting out on the road today too, buddy."

Presley barked.

Before rolling out, Tom checked the steering and the service brake. He placed both hands on the wheel, readying himself for the long drive ahead. The truck wasn't older than twelve years, but sometimes it failed. Not this time.

They left the parking lot right before eight that morning, right on schedule, and Tom reminded himself the storm would soon be far away, and he and Presley would be home in no time with Margaret. Despite his bitterness, the idea of her being home alone made his palms slick. Would she have felt better if Presley had stayed with her instead? When the truck rolled through the parking lot, he left those thoughts behind.

Tom hit the radio and an acoustic guitar radiated out of the speakers together with a female singer. She sang about women's justice and death, a song he had heard before, but this time with changed lyrics.

When they turned out on the main road that morning, the rain fell over Alaska, and it was easy to believe the world was a safe place.

CHAPTER

3

IT DIDN'T TAKE LONG before the rain turned to hail; it sounded like the small heels of a thousand running children.

Tom turned up the volume on the radio, and when he shortly thereafter passed a green road sign that indicated his route, a crazy thought of ditching the plan made him smile. Instead of continuing on the road straight ahead to Elliot Highway, he could steer right onto Steese Highway. From there, he could drive to Chatanika, dump the truck by the road, and then hitch with Presley to Circle, where he could start working at the Circle District Historical Society Museum. If that didn't work out, he would go to Birch Hill, and—

No.

He couldn't afford any mistakes now. What he had to do was to get along with Margaret. To save the house was important. He'd lost a lot of sleep over this the past couple of months. Margaret complained of lack of sleep too, and sometimes it made her nauseous. She wasn't herself anymore. Tom couldn't stand the thought of losing the house he knew Margaret loved. It had belonged to her parents. A secure place where she had created memories and feelings as a child, but after her parents' divorce, she'd lost all that when she had to move away with her mother. After her father's death, many years later, she had inherited the house, and it became a place where she and Tom could expand their lives together. It was supposed to be a place where *they* could create a happy family and live until death tore them apart. That was ten years ago. Not much good had happened since then. All the expenses and bills were about to get them thrown out on the street, and they had been forced to take out more loans to cover the old ones. But Tom couldn't stop trying to save the house. Couldn't stop trying to save their *marriage*. He would do whatever was required.

He had to call her and apologize for his behavior, before they reached Dalton Highway, while it still was possible.

Tom turned down the volume and grabbed the phone from his pocket. Despite the fact that he didn't want to talk while driving, he scrolled down to Margaret and tapped her name. She answered after the first ring.

"I want to apologize," Tom said. "But I'm no magician, Maggie. You have to trust me on this one. Once I'm home, I promise to take you downtown. We'll go to the place you love, The Crepery, or whatever the heck it's called. How does that sound? Or what if I bring home a pepperoni pizza and a couple of Barq's Root Beers with me? I'll get some good money for this job. It will cover some of the bills. Not *all* of them. But *most* of them. Alright? It's the best I can do for now."

"I don't know," she answered, but together with her voice, came a scraping and banging.

Tom pulled the phone away from his ear as if it burned. "What's all that noise?"

"I'm packing."

"Packing?" Tom raised his eyebrows. "For what?"

A thundering noise from Margaret's side made the phone crackle with static. "I called Mom back after you left," she said. "We decided that it would be better if—"

"You're *leaving*?"

The phone line went silent for a couple of seconds, as if a death sentence had been announced for them both.

"Answer me," Tom said. "*Why* are you leaving?"

"All this is tearing me apart," she answered in a low voice. "What more do you want me to say?"

Heat surged up Tom's neck, leaving red splotches. The blood inside him boiled. "Tearing *you* apart? What about *me*? Don't you think—"

"This is the reason why I'm going! I need a rest from all these discussions. From all this fighting. I need to—"

"Rest? Rest is all you do! I'm the only one who tries to get everything worked out. And what do *you* do? All you do is complain! Complain like a fucking child that—"

The line went quiet for a short moment, and Tom was left with a vague buzzing in the background. Silent moments like this never meant any good news.

"I'm sorry," Tom said. "I didn't mean it."

Margaret took a deep breath, lowered her voice, and said, "Mom is driving me back on Monday. I will see how I feel by then. How *you* are feeling by then. Maybe I'll stay even longer."

"Even longer?" Tom laughed a short one. "What have you two talked about?"

"It doesn't matter now."

"It doesn't matter?" Tom gritted his teeth and increased the gas. The trees next to the road flew by like the blade of a circular saw. "It matters to me! Don't you love me anymore?"

"This isn't about loving you, Tom," Margaret said, tears in her throat. "This is about something else. I'm not myself right now. I need to take a break from our home. From *us*. From everything around. I'll explain more when you get back home."

The same thought that had occurred minutes before, now hit Tom again and made him laugh again. "What if I never come home again? Have you ever thought about that? What if—"

"Stop it!" A double knock on the door made her pull the phone away and tell the visitor to wait. "I'm sorry. I need to hang up now. Mom's here. I'll give you a call—" The phone started to blip. Her voice hacked back to him, as if she were a robot trying to speak a futuristic language. When the line, a second later, was taken over by a beep, Tom pulled the phone away from his ear and watched the signal strength diminish from the phone's display.

He sighed and put the phone on the seat next to Presley.

"She picked the witch over me again, Presley."

Presley barked a short one.

"Yeah, buddy. She did. She fucking did."

It was then that it materialized out of nowhere: the rectangular maroon welcome sign (with a dirt colored tree in the middle). The sign stood along the road's edge with the support of three coarse, wooden pillars on each side. The corner of the sign was adorned with colorful fireweed, and in the center, was the shape of Alaska. The sign read, "Welcome to the James Dalton Highway" and under that, "Gateway to the Arctic - the Road to Prudhoe Bay".

This was it for Tom, the start of the road, but for some others, the end of it. Highways around the world could be considered a place for bustling people seeking the meaning of life. Some were searching for some kind of value-creating ideals, where dreams and freedom struck themselves free as great birds in the raw air and where love had no restrictions. Did those kinds of places even exist in reality?

He sighed.

For Tom, trucking, as a job, had at first been a release of spirit where he could breathe and see the world's spectacular landscapes without thinking about everyday needs. But when stress was added to the picture, it instead became *work*, a nine-to-five-thing (when he didn't have to work overtime), where he couldn't wait until he got home again. And fifteen years later, he still hadn't changed jobs. What difference would it make?

He turned up the radio again, but all he was met with was a constant crackle. He tried to change the station but nothing happened. "Perfect," he sighed. "So no fucking radio either. This is gonna be a fun trip, a great one!"

He needed a smoke already, but he had to wait until the hail stopped.

Tom released the gas and continued on the road. For a long time, the scent of the boreal forest seeped through the truck's air vents along with the smell of wet cement. A chain of green and gold trees followed the road as far as he could see. But with the hail mixed into the scene, everything smoothed out like an abstract painting. In some places, the forest had an overgrown look, melting from separate bushes into waves of trees and ferns, while other parts consisted of mossy tree trunks and God only knew what.

In front of them, a dense fog of silence grew, swallowing the mountain peaks. The wind howled against the truck's windshield. It was a long way to go. But if he maintained the same speed all the way to Prudhoe Bay, they would, at least, arrive before midnight.

CHAPTER

4

THE FIRST GAS STATION came after pump station number six at Yukon Crossing. Pump number six was the last pump station—but the first for Tom—from Prudhoe Bay that shot the black oil through the long pipes like a single, fat straw next to the road. The pipeline was the only reason people travelled on Dalton Highway. Without it, nothing would have existed out there, nothing more than the wildlife itself. The pipes went from Prudhoe Bay down to Valdez, the PS12 Marina terminal. It was a long stretch filled with tons of heavy metal pieces from the 1970s.

Next to the gas station was a camp station that offered some food, lodging, and even a few gifts. Tom could buy something for Margaret in there, but did she deserve it?

No.

He had to save the money.

Tom parked the hard-humming death machine by a nostalgic-looking gas pump, which couldn't have been modified since they placed it there ages ago. The clouds were a wavy darkness by now, like the underside of a raven, and the hail had reverted to rain again, which sparkled down on the area as if it was Judgment Day. The dank smell of wet concrete and soil mixed itself with the splashes of fuel and oil from the ground.

His lungs craved some smoke. But it wasn't the right place for it. Was it ever the right time for anything?

He walked up beside the gas pump as the rain pounded against his cap and raincoat. He detested wearing the raincoat since it always made him sweaty. Next time he went out, he would abandon it in the truck no matter how bad the weather was. Best of all would be to throw the coat away so he never would have to see it again. But he had received the coat from Margaret as a wedding present a couple of years ago, and it would hurt her if he threw it out. Maybe he should have.

Next to the fuel pumps sat a plastic jug filled with piss. It could have been there for ages. But he had seen worse human influence on the roads before. Better piss than shit, blood or parts of roadkill. Some truckers behaved like animals when they were on a mission, as if they owned the roads and everything else along with it. It wasn't unusual for some truckers to even fuck whores while they had wives at home.

When the refueling was finished, and Tom was back in the truck, the rain dripped off him and made his seat wet. He ripped off the raincoat and hurled it on the backpack. It could lay there and rot. He didn't care anymore.

Tom turned to Presley. "You don't want to go out and take a pee, do you?"

Presley lay still on the seat giving him an innocent stare.

"As I thought. Maybe next stop."

Tom started the truck and, within a minute, the wheels were rolling again toward Prudhoe Bay, and like a tired kid, Presley fell asleep from the truck's jarring movements and light bumps. A dog's silence conveyed his platonic, hidden undertone. It wasn't anything like a woman's silence, which could mean something more. Sometimes, Presley responded to Tom's voice with a short bark, an innocent look, or occasional snore. Other than that, the dog wasn't much company. But he was still *good* company. And he would be, at least for a little longer.

CHAPTER

5

THE WILDERNESS CONTINUED LIKE a never-ending, low-budget movie trailer, where Tom played the lead role. Toppled pines and cracked tree peaks signaled the cruelties of nature. To the east, where new trees grew, the forest thrived, and to the west, eroded, rugged cliffs with jagged branches broke up the landscape. The road seemed to blend all four seasons into one. In some places, the grass grew paler than a tennis ball, while other parts of the field looked frozen, a bit bumped and ossified, perhaps destroyed by harsh winds or greedy lumberjacks. Whatever the reason, it wasn't like other parts of Alaska; all possible colors had been mixed together like nature's national flag. In one way, it all seemed too perfect, in another, it seemed as if infinite dangers tumbled around the wild terrain, hidden in mythical tracks with foredoomed stories.

Then, as quick as a finger snap, the rain stopped. Tom turned his head from one window to the other. How could it stop so fast? His curiosity almost made him miss a red car parked at an angle, partially on the road. The car glittered from the rain and the sunshine that peeked through the clouds as they changed directions. The car had a black oblong car top carrier on top and looked to be headed on a typical camping trip. But it sat teetering towards the ditch. From the distance, sunlight reflected off the open passenger door window.

Tom raised his eyebrows as he got closer. He could have continued along the road, away from the car, but the situation made his stomach tingle with a curious dread. Something wasn't right. The passenger door stood open as if someone had left the car in a hurry. But where could a person go from there? There was nothing but crooked trees and small bushes pointing skyward.

"What's going on here, buddy?"

No human was in sight. Not even a dog. It was all quiet, as if time had forgotten the place, but it still had a superficial vulnerability.

"Fuck." Tom slowed his speed even more and glanced at the digital clock in the truck before deciding what to do. Did he really have time to check out the car?

No.

He took a hard look at the sight. But what if someone was hurt inside it? He couldn't let it slide so easily. He had to do *something*.

Tom bit his lip until a taste of iron grew in his mouth. A quick look inside the car couldn't hurt. Could it?

He parked the truck in front of the car and gave the side mirror a quick look. Still no one in sight. Could the driver have slipped into the forest to get rid of something shady? Tom shook his head. If so, who would leave such an expensive car in the middle of nowhere without locking it first?

A cold tension picked at Tom's insides. He looked around again for any clues. The forest was neither dense nor deep in the distance; it was easy to see right through it until it was overtaken by the surging shadows further in. Nobody would go so far without a good reason. But if someone was *in* there, the sparse nature would still reveal them, even as a silhouette.

"Alright, buddy," Tom said and turned to Presley. "Let me see what's going on out there. Don't drive away while I'm out, okay?" He ruffled the dogs head and squeezed out a nervous laugh before opening the door. It had, throughout the years, become part of his job as a truck driver to also act as a somewhat freelance road detective, without getting paid. Most truckers didn't care about what happened on the road as long as it didn't affect them; a few still had a heart, though. Tom wanted to be one of them.

He hopped out into the temporarily dry weather as a cold breeze passed by, making him shudder. He moved closer to the red car and still, with no one in sight, he gave a quick glance through the windshield.

Empty.

He walked around to the already open passenger door and poked his head inside. It smelled of rubber and citrus. The decor was in white leather and still had that new car smell, like someone had just driven it off the lot an hour ago. On the driver's seat lay a phone with earbuds. The music pounded in the car's interior. The car keys, still hanging from the ignition, had a metal keyring with a moose on it. Could the car belong to a hunter? Tom turned to the forest. The landscape wasn't good enough for any sort of hunting at this spot, and there were no signs of rifles or hunting gear in the car. Tom bent further inside. On the floor, under the driver's seat, lay a brown wallet and a full bottle of Coke. He put his knee on the passenger's seat as the leather squeaked with his movement. He bent over to the driver's seat, supporting himself on the steering wheel, and picked up the wallet. It was big and fat and leather, with a couple of 50s that stuck out from the top. The person who had dropped it must have been aware of it.

Tom squinted. How much money could be in there?

His mouth went dry. He glanced through the back window of the car, where the sun revealed itself for a couple of seconds before disappearing behind a group of cotton clouds. He licked his lips and lowered his gaze to the wallet again. Would the owner, whoever it was, even notice if Tom pulled out the two 50s? With the money hanging outside like that, they could have fallen out anytime or anywhere. Whoever owned both the car and the wallet, that person sure had more money than Tom had ever had. If Tom took it, the money would at least come to *some* benefit. What did he have to lose?

With a slow and steady movement, like a surgeon in an operating room, Tom pulled out the two 50s; his heart banged hard in his chest. But with the bills, out came a note that swirled down to the passenger's floor. He stared at it for a second with big cartoon-eyes, before he bent down and snatched up the note. It said: "666 KM THROUGH HELL." Tom frowned. What did that mean? Just then, a truck tore past the car window, making him jump and bang the back of his head against the roof of the car. His pulse pounded like a jackhammer in his throat, and the skin on his face heated. Where had the damn truck come from? It had almost given him a heart attack.

"You fucking idiot!" Tom tried to shout, but nothing but an incoherent stuttering came out of him. He tried to swallow, but it was like a jagged stone rolled down his throat. He took a deep breath. Alright. He had done what he could do here. He couldn't be any more help. And without any phone signal out there, he couldn't even call the police about the car. But even if he *could*, would he? What he needed to do was get back to his own truck, and back on the road, before someone else happened. Tom still had a mission to complete of his own, a mission he couldn't afford to fail. He couldn't let anything affect him.

What are you waiting for?

Tom threw the billfold back where he had found it, stuffed the money in his jeans pocket and backed away from the car without touching anything else. He walked straight back to his truck with shaking legs. The rushing sound from the passing rig that had almost scared him to death, and it still pounded and vibrated in his ears.

You idiot.

Before entering his truck, he squeezed his eyes tight and stared out at the wilderness. Something couldn't be right out there, and whatever it was, it made him sweaty and thirsty.

But right now he had more important things to take care of.

CHAPTER

6

ONE HUNDRED DOLLARS RICHER, Tom headed to Prudhoe Bay. After passing a group of wild deer, whose desperation had led them to new, unexplored fields, he, once again, started to think about Margaret. He would never tell her what he had done back there by the car, even if it was for the best for both of them. Sometimes a partner had to close their eyes and mouth in a relationship to avoid further complications. Tom had done it for a long time now. He had to do *something* if their relationship was going to work again. There were no more choices to make, no more cards to pull out, no more shortcuts to take. Their monopoly tokens had passed Go over and over again, and it was time to either end the relationship or repair it for good, with or without the witch by their side.

The group of deer tripped along the road in pursuit of autumn's food, unaware of the danger right next to them, like a big, heavy, murder machine on wheels. They walked around the desolate and sterile place, which may or may not have ample meals buried under thick layers of soil or even in some wild plants nearby. One little failure and they could end up as meatloaf. But their mentality was different from humans. They took the time as it came and solved problems when needed. Humans did the opposite.

The possibility of rain hid somewhere far away, and the fog still crept along the road. Tom had to be careful. Cracks and holes deep as the tires were covered with dirt and debris. They were difficult to note and even harder to avoid at high speed.

His back ached and his ass was numb from sitting too long. His lungs, and even his head, screamed for a cigarette by now. He needed to enjoy one before he lost his mind.

When they reached the sign for the Arctic Circle, at mile 115, Tom slowed the loaded truck and parked in a pull-off. Outside the truck, he placed a smoke between his lips and lit it with his trusty, eagle Zippo. A thing he could trust.

Behind the Arctic Circle sign was the entrance to an overlook. The overlook revealed an area that opened out towards the deep boreal forest and mountains, so large it was surreal. The fog slithered like a silent snake that snuck around the trees.

Two bulletin boards stood by the railing of the overlook. Tom went along with Presley to the first board. It contained park rules, where the picnic areas were, and how to get to them. But what kind of maniac brought a picnic all the way out here? The bulletin board also had a yellow and red warning note about bears, moose, and other dangerous animals. It was vital not to enrage or feed them, or else, they could become bear food themselves.

Tom inhaled the cigarette smoke as his lungs expanded with the poison.

Dozens of birds sang above them in an uneven melody, and Presley sniffed around and peed on the already dewy grass. They went along to the other bulletin board next to the first one. Tom's eyes went wide and a heavy bolt of fright struck him for the first time that day. The bulletin board was covered with pictures. Most of them were portraits ranging from younger, high-school-aged girls to older, bearded men with serious faces and hunter rifles by their side. They all said MISSING above them. One said: "HAVE YOU SEEN MY BROTHER, JACOB WILKINS?" together with a photo of a young man with wavy hair and an Anchorage Glacier Pilots cap. Another note stated nothing more than, "666." Tom scratched his scruff, and his thoughts began to spin. "What the hell is this?"

Presley remained silent.

The handwritten note from the wallet had the same numbers as the note in front of him.

On most of the fliers was the missing person's name, nickname, age, or where they were last seen.

A dying breeze passed by and brought a damp smell with it.

Tom couldn't take his eyes off the photos. Some were dated less than a couple of weeks ago, some decades ago. On some, relatives offered large rewards to whoever found them. One flier even offered a one hundred thousand dollar reward.

Tom gasped. For one hundred thousand dollars, he could keep his eyes a little more open at the edge of the road. With that much money he could pay all the bills, buy a new pickup, renovate the house, and even take Margaret on a vacation. He enjoyed the thoughts. But it didn't take long before he got pulled back into reality again, where the face of a missing woman looked at him from the bulletin board. She had long, blonde hair falling in big curls against her shoulders. Her face was filled with freckles. She couldn't be any older than her twenties. Had he seen her somewhere else? Maybe she reminded him of Margaret when she had been that age. The woman had been wearing a white dress when she went missing in October of last year. She had last been seen at the border of Ray River, alone in her car.

Tom shook. "What's going on out here, Presley?"

The dog whined.

A note at the bottom of the bulletin board, which looked as if it came from a government website, stated Alaska had the most missing persons within the U.S.— and also the fewest number of recoveries.

Tom grimaced. It wasn't really what he needed to know right now. He threw the burning cigarette on the wet concrete and stamped on it. He had lost the taste for smoking. What kind of place was it? What kind of *road*?

He turned around looking for something, a sign, a voice, anything that would break his thoughts. Nothing. So many people seemed to go missing out here in the middle of nowhere, but where did they all go? His pulse hit a few beats harder than usual, and it didn't take long before he returned to a childhood memory. Back then, a serial killer had been active not far from where he lived with his parents. The killer had brought his victims to the Alaskan wilderness where he had released them like animals, only to hunt them down again like a predator. Could there be a copycat out there somewhere?

You're being ridiculous.

Tom glared at the forest around him. The missing people couldn't have vanished into smoke. But what was the likelihood there was another serial killer out there? He frowned. If not a serial killer, there were still a lot of animals around. Animals in Alaska were often guilty of mass destruction on farms and around the towns, but sometimes they were accused of human disappearances as well. Could it be such a simple case? If so, the police would at least be able to find an arm, a leg, maybe even a head. But had they found anything at all? The bulletin board said nothing about that.

Tom glanced at Presley who stood next to him staring at the forest with his tongue hanging out. Could Presley be capable of such violence?

Tom swallowed hard. If they left now, they would soon be at Prudhoe Bay.

Tom patted Presley's back, dropped his eyes from the bulletin board, and walked back to the truck with heavy legs.

Whatever had happened out there, Tom didn't want to become part of it.

In the warm truck, they would be safe.

At least for a while.

CHAPTER

7

TOM DROVE PAST GOBBLERS Knob and continued at the recommended speed of 50 mph toward pump station five. He wanted to drive faster but didn't want to be reckless.

The gloomy, quiet fog had crept further toward the road. A few whining shrieks sounded from the air pressing against the windshield. How much further?

Tom sighed and massaged the back of his neck with sweaty fingers. Being a truck driver meant physical problems from the first trip. It didn't matter whether the trucking companies installed thousand-dollar seats since the problem came from how long someone had to sit in them. It wasn't uncommon for drivers to develop chronic neck, back, and knee problems, which later became unbearable. Tom had all three now and then, and it was worse during winter. But he had, throughout the years, gotten used to it, despite needing to see a doctor. He didn't have the money to be running to the doctor's all the time. And who knew how much the medicine would cost if he needed any? He had to suck it up, even if the vibrations from the truck came as damage to the spinal cord. But the most intense problem had always been the mental part: the constant stress and inactivity that gave rise to everything from cardiovascular disease to depression and heavy drug abuse. Tom had been on the edge of falling victim to the pitfalls many times. Everyone out on the road had a more significant risk of marital problems and divorce. Tom, himself, was a living example. How many more problems could work cause before it would be enough? He had to change jobs. One day, he would have to.

After Gobblers Knob, he traversed the Jim River area, which was a long lake surrounded by high mountains. The ongoing fog and the unending forest stared at him from above and touched him from behind. Farther on, by Grayling Lake, a couple of kayaks were floating into the fog like dead fish, but there was nobody in them.

Tom ran his hand through his hair. He must have mistaken the kayaks for something else. If he hadn't, there must be a logical reason they were empty.

He squeezed his fingers more tightly against the wheel. He didn't have time for anymore nonsense now. All he needed to think about was getting to Prudhoe Bay before midnight. Tomorrow night, he would be home again, and everything would be as usual. He would drink a beer, listen to the radio, and get a good night's sleep.

Tom scratched Presley on his head and behind his ears, but the dog wanted to sleep.

Between South Fork Koyukuk and its glittering lake, a green travel bus had stopped next to the road. Some signs of humans. Good. A group of tourists had gone outside to take pictures and to stretch their legs. Some even seemed to be looking for some kind of excitement or anything else unusual out there. Good luck.

Tom laughed a short one.

Presley sat up and watched the bus and the group of people with delight. He jerked his tail a few times when the truck drove past. The fun part didn't last long. Presley fell down onto the seat again and back into sleep. The sign of life had come up as quick as it had disappeared.

Close by, a sign said, "oh shit corner!"

Tom read aloud, "Oh shit corner? Why would someone name a damn sign for—" But after the curve it was understandable why someone had placed the sign there. It could have been a weary, local resident, who had had enough of people complaining about the vicious curves. Or maybe it was some humorous soul who wanted to play a joke, but whoever did it, the sign made its point.

The next sign indicated a reduced speed of 10 mph. Tom released the gas to let the engine slow down. That's when the sign for Coldfoot appeared. It was the last place with food and fuel along the road, but it also meant his last contact with civilization. He had no other choice than to stop there. Missing it could leave him stranded along the road further on.

As the speed limit dropped to ten, the vehicle crept along the noisy ground further into the center of Coldfoot. It was a speed limit Tom wanted to break, but it was set at 10 mph for a reason. Why didn't someone do anything about all the road damage?

Tom turned onto a narrow road, which led him into a campsite for passing drivers and adventurous tourists. Rows of wrecked cars stood at the edge of the forest, and several campers were parked bumper to bumper in another row in the center of the clearing. Further down the road was a wooden house.

His stomach grumbled.

Maybe it was a restaurant. It would be best to save the contents of the backpack as long as he could.

Tom drove closer to the wooden house and parked the truck near two others. Even though the place had the look of an abandoned cabin, a silhouette revealed someone was in there.

"Alright, buddy," Tom said. "I'll be back in a couple of minutes."

Presley had to stay in the truck while Tom went to see if the place was even open. If it wasn't, he would have to take from the backpack until he reached Prudhoe Bay.

Out of the truck, Tom narrowed his eyes into the sky. The tall mountain peaks were silhouetted by vague sunlight from behind. Below the mountains, the area was spotted with a few trees retreating in fear. Elongated shadows stretched across the ground. The fog kept its distance. Birds circled above the trees with screams of warning.

Ravens.

Had they been following him?

Aside from the birds, the area stood quiet. A few breezes forced their way to him in a silent wave. It was like everyone had abandoned their vehicles out there—like they had all run away. Would it be a good idea to go into the cabin, or would he find a group of missing, dead people in there?

Tom frowned.

Get yourself together.

A quick meal, and then he would be back on his way to Prudhoe Bay.

He walked toward the house. A movement in the shadows by the porch, close to the entrance, revealed someone in a rocking chair. It could have been a scarecrow if the person hadn't been smoking.

Tom continued up the slanted, wooden staircase. Wooden railings ran straight up to the porch, and the color of both the stairs and the house had long fled its original shade. It had its charm, but it looked to be a dangerous place for some.

There, by the entrance, sat an old beardy man with a cigarette in his mouth. The old man wore a grubby unbuttoned shirt, revealing a chest filled of curly white hair. His jeans had spots of motor oil, and on his head he wore a cap that had seen better days.

"Your dog?" The old man asked with a heavy, whiskey voice, while he nodded toward the truck. "Seems to be waiting for you already."

Tom threw a glance back to the side window of the truck and laughed a short one. "That's Presley. He's alright."

The old man raised one of his bushy eyebrows. "Presley? You named a dog after a *singer*?"

Tom nodded. "One of the greatest."

The old man blew out a cloud of smoke as his eyes wandered up the white powdery mountain tops. "Wow."

Tom smiled and made to pass the fellow, when a hand against his stomach stopped him.

"George," the old man stated and outstretched a massive and fumbling hand, with more of those white hairs on its knuckles. "George Goldman. But you can call me George. Or Mister Goldman. The choice is yours."

Tom shook the man's hand. "Tom Richards."

"You got a big truck over there, son. How far are you going?"

Tom nodded in the direction of his destination. "Over to Prudhoe Bay. I'm looking to be there by midnight."

George squinted and stretched out a red cigarette package with Marlboros. "You smoke?"

Tom hesitated. This man could have done anything with those cigarettes: put them in bleach, poured poison in them, anything.

"Thank you," Tom said, "but I've quit."

George pulled back the package with a huff. "You from the lower 48, son?"

"Fairbanks."

In the same moment, a group of birds passed above them and screamed as if their wings were on fire.

"See, they are fleeing from where you are going," George said, quiet for a few seconds. "*That's* a warning."

Tom squeezed his eyes shut. "A warning?"

"Those bristle-thighed curlews are one of Alaska's few endemic vulnerable species. Beautiful birds, if you ask me. They can only be found in two different places here in Alaska: by the Yukon River and on the Seward Peninsula. Around this time they make their autumn migration southwest of Japan. Sometimes farther away to Hawaii or the Marshall Islands in Oceania." He took a break to inhale the smoke from the cigarette. "But you heard their screams, son. They are *frightened*. Frightened of what's out there."

Tom glanced at the birds and then back at George. "And ... what *is* out there?"

George followed the birds until they disappeared into the sky as if he glanced away from reality for a second. "There are many stories about this particular road," he said. "People think Russia sold us Alaska because they found themselves in some kind of economic crisis. Back then, Mr. Seward spoke of something he didn't specifically acknowledge. When the Russians sold Alaska to us, they already *knew* what was out there. Do you understand me, son? They sold us the damn place because they already knew!" He took another deep breath and shook his head. "The Russians wanted to get away from it. To protect their *own* people. It became Seward's icebox after all, as people were saying. The *dead* icebox. If I were you, I would turn that truck around and never come back here."

Tom swallowed. The last words rang like the clang of a heavy, dark church bell.

"Some say, even the man himself, Dalton, met the true evil on these roads," George continued. "They say it happened when he oversaw the pipeline building. I'm sure you've seen the pipeline. And I'm convinced that's the main reason you're even here." George's voice lowered as he leaned forward in the chair. It creaked with every movement he made. "The wilderness has many secrets, son. Do yourself a favor - turn around while you still can."

Tom shrugged. "I don't have any choice."

George tipped his hat with a smile. "A man has to do what a man has to do, right?"

"And sometimes," Tom said, "a man has to do the opposite of what he really wants."

George's smile faded. "But remember, son, when you leave here today, there's no longer any service out there in the bush. Nobody to call. Nobody to help. And you do best to stay inside the truck when the darkness falls. Whatever happens on the outside, *always* stay inside the truck. Do you hear me?"

Tom swallowed hard again, grabbed the oval, wooden handle next to George, and gave it a yank. Before he entered the restaurant, he said, "I hear you, George, but I prefer my dog to pee on the outside."

8

THE WOMAN BEHIND THE checkout looked at Tom with a big smile and without blinking. "Do you want to die, sir?" she asked. "Special deal today, only $9.99."

Tom wrinkled his eyebrows and laughed a brief one. "I-I'm sorry," he said. "What did you just say?"

"I asked if you'd like some pie, sir. It's a special deal today. We have both—"

"No, no." He laughed. "A burger is fine. I'll take one of those…" He studied the menu. "A reindeer burger, please, with a side of onion rings."

"Anything to drink?"

"Coke, please."

The woman gave him a Coke from the refrigerator behind her. "$19.99, please."

Tom fished out the money he had stolen from the red car. The woman took the cash, stared at it for a second as if she was analyzing it, and then put it in the register.

Tom was sweating.

"Please take a seat", the woman said, giving back the change with a smile. "I'll come out with your order in a couple of minutes."

Tom nodded, grabbed the Coke, and took a seat close by.

She knows you stole them.

Tom got sweaty. He opened the coke. Did she?

No.

He took a sip and looked around. Some low music seeped from a hidden speaker. The walls were adorned with paintings, aging wallpaper, and a moose head. But where was everybody? He was the only customer. The only one he had seen outside the restaurant was that old man, George.

Tom took another sip. *George.* Who was he? Tom couldn't let go of what George had said to him. Could there be any truth in it? The old man must be senseless, a lunatic, an escaped mental patient, convinced of his own crazy stories. How long had it been since the old man had visited any real sort of civilization, except for this restaurant in the middle of nowhere?

He sighed.

Total isolation could knock any man to the edge of insanity. It could cause anyone to believe their own lies until there were no longer any lies to be told. No, he couldn't believe him. The old man had cabin fever.

Tom yawned. His eyelids became heavier and his muscles too. He gave a thought to Presley. The dog needed a break too, and he considered giving him some food and water when he got back to the truck. Perhaps he wanted to pee as well. Tom searched around for a toilet himself. He was just about to get up to find one when the plate was served in front of him.

"Have a nice meal!" The woman said with that big smile again.

She fucking knows.

Tom nodded back with a smile. What difference would it make if she did? The smell of a warm burger and onion rings made his taste buds jump for joy. He could wait a few more minutes to piss. And when he had finished both eating and pissing, he would take care of Presley. But he also needed to fuel the tank one last time before leaving. He couldn't forget that.

The music continued to seep.

A wind whistled on the outside.

Tom was busy chewing when another sound made him look up. It was the sound of laughter. The chef, a small man with bushy eyebrows, was now standing next to the woman behind the cashier. They both glanced at Tom.

No.

The chef whispered something in the woman's ear that made her burst into more giggles.

Tom solidified.

Don't you get it? Don't you get what they've done?

Tom lowered his gaze to the plate as the blood drained from his face. A sudden nausea flushed through him. He pushed away the plate and spat out the food. Then he rose quickly. The chair almost tipped over, but he saved it.

"Is something wrong, sir?" the woman asked.

Don't let them get you!

"Sir?"

Tom didn't answer her, but instead ran straight to the door. He stumbled toward the slanted, wooden staircase, as nausea intruded. He glanced sideways, but the rocking chair was empty.

Empty.

Tom was shadowed from the sun, which hid behind dark rain clouds. Clouds that were, once again, taking over the sky. The mountains stood at attention, and the dark silhouettes of angular tree peaks shone, as the light snuck through where it could.

He hurried to his truck, swung the door open, climbed in, and sat down with a thump.

Presley swished his tail and greeted him by licking his face thousands of times.

Tom turned his cheek. "Enough!"

His pulse banged in his throat. He closed the door and started the motor, when a reflection in the side mirror caught his attention.

Tom's eyes widened.

It was a man in white, with something sharp in his hand.

The chef.

"Sir?" the chef shouted.

What the hell are you waiting for?

The chef came closer.

Tom's legs weakened. He started breathing heavily.

Go!

"Excuse me, sir?"

Tom floored the gas pedal, and a cloud of sand and dust filled the side mirrors.

CHAPTER

9

TOM RICHARD'S BODY WAS shaking, but he still tried to keep the recommended speed limit, despite the sky now resembling a thick layer of bubbling mud, and, from time to time, it threw down such heavy rain the truck was difficult to handle. Even though he was on his way to Prudhoe Bay, the place where Tom could relax with a beer in his hand, he couldn't prevent his thoughts from spinning like a wheel rolling downhill.

Don't you get they tried to poison you?

He rubbed his furrowed eyebrows as he tried to focus. He couldn't let go of what had happened at the restaurant.

Tom tried to take a deep breath when it hit him. They had tried to kill him because of all the unpaid bills. They had been sent out there to catch him alive, because of his incompetency to pay for himself. He needed to get to Prudhoe Bay before the night sky fell. It could be his only way to survive. If he earned his paycheck, things would be back to normal. The only way to get the money was to *earn* it. He wasn't a criminal. He had morals. Theft wasn't an option. No, he couldn't risk it.

Tom took a deep breath and glanced in the side mirror. There were no traces of people, animals, or vehicles around. He was safe now. His breath hissed out.

But how far away could the oil field be? He had been driving for hours, gone past Wiseman and a few more pump stations, not sure of where he now was. The pipeline still followed the side of the road as innocently as it had done the whole time.

Even though Tom drove with the windshield wipers at the highest speed, he had to squint to detect the road signs. Everything blurred in front of him. The rain bouncing against the truck sounded like a tommy gun.

A few miles east, thunder broke loose as a lightning bolt struck like a bomb detonating a city. The sky exploded in a quick flashbulb of yellow light. The bright disappeared into the emptiness, while the pixelated flash pattern remained. Sound waves twisted into a dark, coarse, rattling funnel cloud, which thousands of years ago might have been seen as a warning to humanity but was now regarded as an everyday message to stay inside. Or at least to take cover.

The shadows from the forest reached over the truck and made imprints inside the cabin, while the mountains stood like guards in the open countryside behind the trees farther in. In the rain and fog, the mountains stood silent, as if they were observing the road from a distance.

Tom picked up the map from the backpack, where he found Wiseman with his shaking finger. How far away from Wiseman were they? Did it even matter? They wouldn't get there any faster anyway. Did he even need the map? It couldn't be too difficult to find the way if he followed the road signs. The main road was easy to find. The minor roads that led from it were often private roads. He just had to maintain focus and avoid making any mistakes.

Drive, you moron!

From nowhere came a wheezing and scraping metallic sound on the right side of the truck. Seconds later, came a heavy slam.

Tom winced and looked through the side window with wide eyes.

Presley sat up. The dog pressed his face against the glass.

Tom's mouth went dry as he slowed his speed. He tried to see any damage in the side mirror. Nothing. He had to stop and see what happened. In the worst-case scenario, a wheel could have been damaged or even exploded. But something made him push the gas instead of the brakes. There was something that reflected in the side mirror. Whether it was a car, truck, or motorcycle, it came after him.

They found you.

"*No.*" Tom tightened his grip on the steering wheel and pushed the gas harder.

Presley whimpered. It didn't take long before his whimpering grew to a heavy whining, as if he was in pain. The dog sat up on the seat, and his whining pitched higher. His eyes were attached to the windshield.

Tom glanced at him. "Hey, lay down!"

Presley didn't.

They're out there. Drive!

Within seconds, Presley's whining morphed into dark growling. He put his paws up on the dashboard then pressed them against the windshield. He panted, his chest heaving, and his tongue dangled out of his mouth.

They're getting closer.

"Hey!" Tom couldn't keep his focus on the dog anymore. He had to maintain eye contact with the road. "Get down from there!"

But Presley stayed still, with his ears pointed upward, his dark growling continued.

Tom hit the seat next to him with his right palm as a warning. He searched for the dog's leash with his hand. "I said get down from there, Presley!"

Presley growled, and in the next second, his barking filled up the cab like a speaker on full blast. His saliva splattered all over the inside of the windshield, and the sound waves from his barks drilled through Tom's ears.

Tom gave a quick look at the side window, where the reflection still appeared, and then stretched over the seat to grab the leash that lay on the floor.

The truck forced its way through the fog at high speed.

When Tom found the leash, he snatched it hard and pulled the barking dog down from the dash. The moment Presley got back on his seat, one of the air pressure gauges dropped to the bottom. And without warning, the radio blasted at max volume, making Tom's heart triple its beats. The hair on his neck stood out like thin, sharp nails. What came out of the radio wasn't music or not even a voice. It was more like the screaming static of an old-school television sign-off.

Tom searched for the off button on the radio as he stared out against the gloomy road ahead and tried to maintain control. "Make them stop! Make them fucking stop!"

Presley trembled and looked up at Tom with his tongue out, whining. He couldn't be silent for a second. His body twisted, and it looked like he wanted to leap from the truck, out into the storm.

The rain slapped the windshield like a violent whip.

In the roaring sound and feeble light, the off button had seemed to vanish. But once his fingertips did locate it, Tom pressed the button with no results.

The shrieking noises from the radio continued together with Presley's barking.

Tom's face flared up. His hands shook. The sweat poured out of him. "Be quiet, Presley! Shut up!"

The noises swarmed through his head like a horde of insects.

"Leave me alone! I will pay the damn bills, do you hear *me*?" Tom closed his fist and gave the radio a hard knock, and the world went silent for a second, except for the pouring rain against the truck.

He gave another quick look in the side mirror, but it was in that moment it happened: the truck's right wheels slid over the edge of the road, and Tom gasped and stood on the brakes. In a staggering panic, he tightened his grip even more and steered all he could to the left, toward the middle of the road, but it was too late; the truck's rear end skidded over the wet ground, and despite having the seat belt on, the high speed threw him into the door. Something in his shoulder snapped, and he dropped his grip of the steering wheel. His foot slid off the brake. Presley was thrown down on the floor with a bark. The dog curled into a tight ball. The lights on the panel gleamed in all possible colors, as warning signals shouted from the dash. The gasket broke and rolled, and an anxious muffling noise appeared from somewhere in the back of the truck. The wheels shouted with a whining screaming against the soaked road. The left front wheels struck down and Tom flew forward, chest first, against the steering wheel. It caused his teeth to smack together. He forced his right hand forward, gripping the steering wheel, but he had lost all control.

Presley continued his frightened barking from the floor. He shook with violent spasms as the truck bounced through the gloomy landscape. The force pressed Tom's body against the door again and seconds of unlimited fear sliced through him like sharp razor blades. The grey trees in the fog swept past the windows. They came closer. And it could only mean one thing—they were about to drive off the road.

The last two tires in the back of the truck slipped against the ditches. A metallic sound surfaced as the motor fought in a rebellion. The back part of the truck clanked with a throbbing and shadows swirled about the ceiling.

The truck rolled to the left side of the road with a powerful bang from the rear. Tom was thrown against the ceiling, but the belt snapped him back.

The truck fought with vibrating and rattling movements farther into the wet terrain. Equipment flew around the cab. The panel continued to blink multi-colors. The radio shouted its last noises, and rough, bouncing movements brought the truck forward through the unknown. It rolled over bushes and young trees, ripping and tearing, sounding like a jammed wood chipper. The front of the truck forced its way through scraping branches. Despite it all happening in a few seconds, in Tom's head, it took place over several painful minutes. His survival instincts kicked in, searching for options. There were none left. Fate decided what would happen next.

For a short moment, his sight blurred, and it was like he floated in the air.

Then the front of the truck was pushed inward, and everything went black.

CHAPTER

10

WHY DIDN'T SHE EVER listen to him?

"It's for your own safety," his mother told him. "It will make you feel better, Tom. I promise. At least give it a try, honey."

He gave her a look as if she didn't understand a thing. "I already have, Mom! Last week! Do you remember?"

Why did he have to fight with her about it? Why could she never listen to him?

His mother stared at him for a few seconds with her lips pressed into a pale line. "Then give it a second chance, Tom Richards! You're going in no matter if you want to or not! Do you understand me, young man?"

He sighed. There was no point arguing with her anymore. Instead, he went out in the shivering rain and slammed the car door.

"I will be waiting for you here in the car!" his mother shouted, but the shut doors made her voice sound subdued. Of course, she would wait for him in the car. He was only ten years old. He couldn't walk all the way home on his own. Especially not in the rain.

Tom raised his head to the white-colored house with a sign. There she stood, Miss Paterson, as if she had waited on him forever. The gravel drive ran between the two of them, flanked on each side by mixed flowers of all colors: red roses and purple lavender. In the rain it all smelled refreshing. The rain at least kept the insects away.

Miss Paterson had dressed herself in a decent polo shirt, buttoned tight around her neck. Despite the fact that she had to be somewhere around fifty, she wore a slim, dark skirt which made her legs shine white like cow's milk. She had a golden barrette in the shape of a beetle clipped in her long, curly, red hair.

"Hurry, Tom!" Miss Paterson said as her smile exposed her ivory and excellent teeth. "The rain will make you cold! I've got some cookies and hot chocolate waiting for us in here!"

Tom walked to her and didn't turn around to the car once. He followed Miss Paterson inside the house, hung his jacket by the door, and took off his shoes by the entrance. "Aren't you going to let my friend in?" he asked.

Miss Paterson smiled. "Of course, Tom. I'm sorry." She held the door open for a few more seconds. "Are we ready to go?"

Tom nodded.

He tailed her down the stairs like the last time, where those paintings of Winnie the Pooh and Alice's Adventures hung in golden frames on the walls. Once again, they made him smile.

Downstairs had a different look than upstairs. Downstairs was the place where she had her office, the place where she helped children like Tom. Children with "small problems," as his mother explained.

Tom followed her to the same room as he did the previous week. It was simple and white. He had never been in those other two rooms down the hall. What could be in them?

In the middle of her office, stood the same small, round table made of light wood as the time before. Next to one side of the table stood a dark brown chair, while on the other side, stood a bench. Nothing had changed. Nothing except what sat on the table. Now it contained of a cup of hot chocolate and a bowl with some ginger snaps and Fig Newtons. Previously, it had been bananas, apples, and oranges. His dad used to buy cookies every Friday after work, sometimes even ginger snaps and Fig Newtons, but he had preferred to buy Twinkies for Mom and Ding Dongs for Tom. For himself, he purchased a few bottles of IPA, just like he had done the day he died.

Miss Paterson bored her eyes into Tom. "Is everything OK?"

Tom sat down on the sofa without answering.

The room wasn't big at all, not enough space for more than two. It had a narrow window almost at the top of the ceiling. Some floral curtains hung straight down. The rest of the room was pure white.

Miss Paterson took a seat in the chair in front of Tom. "Please have something to eat. And your friend can eat too."

Tom nodded as he took a ginger snap from the bowl even though he wasn't hungry.

"The last time you were here, Tom, I gave you some—homework. How did it go?" She put one hand over the other, and a golden ring exposed her marriage with someone Tom had never met.

Tom dug his right hand into his jeans pocket, retrieving a wrinkled, folded paper. He stretched it over the table.

She took it, looked at it, and formed her lips into a tense bow. Her eyes got big as she nodded to the paper. "Interesting, interesting." But after looking at the paper for a few more seconds, her face transformed into understanding, and her eyes clouded. "Is this … your friend?"

Tom nodded.

Miss Paterson opened her mouth to say something more, but closed it and instead placed the drawing to the side. She took a gulp of her hot chocolate, hummed, and crossed her legs. She grabbed a notebook from the side of the chair and said, "Would you like to talk about her?"

Tom shook his head and pulled into the couch, trying to shrink in size. "She doesn't like when I talk about her."

A worry wrinkle appeared between Miss Paterson's eyebrows. She wrote down some words in her notebook and hummed.

Outside, the rain increased in strength, as a pushing wind made the window whistle.

Tom sat silent for a few seconds staring outside.

Miss Paterson changed her leg position and hummed once again. "What do you think about, Tom?"

Tom looked at her with glazed eyes, and in the same moment, the window blew open, and the rain rushed in and splattered all over the room and on the floor. It didn't take long before it splattered both of them and the table too.

Miss Paterson got up from her chair and knocked her hot chocolate over. She went to the window and tried to close it, but the wind was too fierce.

And the rain continued to hit against Tom's face, over and over again.

PART TWO

CHAPTER

11

TOM RICHARDS WAS WRENCHED from his nightmare and sucked in a breath when cold water splattered against his face. He forced his eyes open, and for a split second, he had no idea where he was. A damp and darkened fog surrounded him as the frigid water seeped through his clothing. He shivered in waves, and his pulse banged in his head like a drumbeat. He tried to move, but his head erupted in a white explosion of dizzy confusion. Every pulse made his neck cramp and eyes blur. His eyes darted around the darkness, his mind filled with an ominous clutter. The day's events blasted through him with a sparkling thunder, one by one, moment after moment.

The road.

The restaurant.

The crash.

The *dog*. Where was Presley?

Ignoring the electric bolt of pain that shot through his body, he stretched his right arm to the passenger side with a wince. "Presley?"

Empty.

No.

An icy tornado of fear forced its way inside his chest and sped his heartbeat toward implosion. He tried getting up again but couldn't move. *Something* held him down, something tight. It had to be the seatbelt. He tried to bite it off with such force his teeth nearly broke. He searched with his cold, shaking fingers for the buckle with another wince. When he found the button, he pushed it as hard as he could, and the belt gave off a creaking sound. Its release felt like an achievement of Harry Houdini. He grabbed the steering wheel but lost his grip when every movement shot blasts of shock and pain through him. The world spun like a centrifuge. The dizziness made him push his hands against his temples as he whimpered out a pathetic sound.

Outside, a shrill sound pierced its way through the pouring rain and past the howling wind.

It was a bark. *Presley's* bark.

Tom's heart bounced in his chest. He leaned against the window beside, and, despite that it was covered with both dirt and hanging branches, he tried to shout for the dog while watching for any movement. But his voice was nothing more than a silent scream. His breath fogged the glass, but that was it. Presley was out there *somewhere*, but all he could see was a gloomy, faint light, provided by the evening sun, that lay behind dark clouds and caused the dense leaves of the trees to give off endless shadows.

He needed light.

He searched with his trembling hands for the key, and when he found it, he twisted it and waited for the headlights to brighten the forest. Nothing happened. No sounds, no lights, not even a warning from the panel appeared. Everything was a thick, inky black.

And the rain continued to spit on him.

Frustration bubbled within him. He had to get out of the truck. *Needed* to get out in the fresh air before he collapsed. Out to Presley. Find him. But Tom's head was about to explode. He was on the edge of paralyzation. He searched for the door handle, hands shaking. He found it and yanked, but the wetness caused his hand to slip off. He gritted his teeth and banged his hand on the window. "Help me! Please! Help … me."

Focus, you prick!

Tom looked around with his eyes wide open. "Who's there?"

Someone started to laugh at him, a dark and hollow laugh.

"Who the hell are you?" Tom shouted. "Show yourself!"

But the laugh disappeared when another bark forced its way through the storm.

"Presley?" Tom said, voice shaking. He had to hurry away from there, hurry to find the dog before someone else did.

With a firmer grip on the handle, Tom rammed his shoulder against the door, and it swung open with a snapping and sparking sound. The movement from his arm, a movement he had made thousands of times before, now sent a burning sensation through his entire body. But he couldn't stop now. He turned his legs out of the cab and moaned.

There was no one outside.

Tom's body hammered in pain, and the rain slammed into him. He gasped for breath as the raw air filled his lungs and made him cough. The smell of burnt metal and gasoline with the mixture of rainy forest smothered him. What if the whole truck was about to explode?

A wave of panic rinsed through him. He couldn't remain there any longer. And without him, Presley would die out there too. No, he couldn't let it happen.

Tom tried to get down from the truck, but small floating dots circulated in the air in front of him. He had to hold a tight grip on the door frame to avoid falling down. When his vision cleared, he glanced at the trees in front of him, where the gloomy darkness obscured everything around. He needed light. Could there be a flashlight in the truck?

He twisted back to the cab and wobbled.

That's when he stiffened; a few feet from him, through the windshield, stuck a rough branch—right into the passenger seat. It could have executed him on the spot. *Or* Presley. His heart now throbbed in a frantic rhythm as if it would jump right out of his mouth. Had the branch hurt his dog? Could Presley have wandered off to die alone as animals often did? The thought made him gasp, and the urge to run straight out in the forest hit him, but first he needed some light.

In frustration, he dug around by the seats as grains of glass stuck into his palm. He yanked his hand away. Searched for what could have been seconds, minutes, hours. But it wasn't until something knocked against his boot as he bent down. It was a flashlight. Another jolt of electrifying pain shot through him. Despite his tensed body, his hands trembled. He managed to get the light to glow in the cabin. His eyes adjusted like an animal's.

Another short bark from the outside made Tom twitch, and this time the bark had more urgency.

The glass pieces from the windshield shone like diamonds on the seat. No blood in sight. He turned the flashlight against the windshield. Besides the massive hole, the rest of the windshield had cracked like a spider web. No blood there either. That was a relief, but he had to get out of the truck before the dog forever disappeared. Or before the truck exploded.

The wind howled through the cab like a bouncing metallic fist against battling cymbals.

Tom clamped his teeth together and lifted the flashlight in front of him. Where had the barks come from? The light struggled its way through the fog.

Nothing in sight. Nothing more than a vague designation of coniferous trees, shrubs, and wild grass. He was lost. But the dog had to be out there *somewhere.*

Get out there, trucker! What are you waiting for?

Tom turned around, his heart almost exploding. "Who's there? I have a weapon! Don't get any closer!" But there was still no one in sight. What did they do to him? His head was spinning, and all those voices made him dizzier. Where did they come from?

He wanted to run away, but he had to take it easy. He moved downward with the help of the outside handle. His legs shook as he reached the overgrown, tangled grass. With his arm out to feel his way in the darkness, he started the search for Presley, but his head still spun round and round. He could fall at any moment, but he had to get it together. It was nothing but a stupid shock.

Tom cupped his hands around his dry mouth and tried to shout for the dog. Presley gave no response. The heartbreaking circumstances rolled out of him like burning coal. He gasped for breath, unsure where to move, and staggered along the front of the truck.

A vibrating click, together with a deep sizzling noise, sputtered from the engine. He plunged his left boot down on a broken fern and lit up the slope against the square truck. The maniacal tree had made a devastating impact to the front. The engine was boiling, and smoke swirled from it, dense and dark.

Tom used the side of the truck for support and followed it all the way back. "Pres… Presley?"

Presley wasn't there either. Tom directed the flashlight forward. The truck had been a savage beast and sabotaged everything in its path. The grass was smashed flat, shrubs were annihilated, and the tires had caused massive ruts in the soft soil. How far from the road could he be? Wherever the road was, the fog now covered it. But if Tom followed the tracks from the wheels, he would get back to the highway in no time. And he would have considered it, if not for another call from Presley. This time, there were several barks in a row, as if the dog hunted something. Or *fled* from something. The blood in Tom's veins turned icy as he worried about the wolves and the bears that prowled the wilderness. Even the moose were dangerous. Also, other people. People who wanted to hurt Tom.

Tom had to find the dog, now.

The tracks behind the truck would be his greatest chance of being rescued. But if he ever wanted to see his dog again, he had to follow Presley's barks—in the opposite direction, right into the forest.

He swallowed hard.

He had no other choices.

Tom staggered away from the truck, going north, and the fog swallowed him whole.

CHAPTER

12

THAT FRIDAY AFTERNOON IN September may have been one of the year's rainiest and most foggy days in Alaska. Leaves filled with rain tipped their load, as long white worms crawled up from beneath the earth, seeking oxygen. Birds hid in the invisible treetops while the smaller animals crawled underneath for protection. The moss and cones were drenched by the downpour, while the hollows in the tree trunks filled to the maximum, forcing the insects out over the edge like a sinking boat. Everything in nature searched for protection when the storms came. And the darkness of the night slithered closer.

Tom had to find Presley before darkness fell over Alaska. Before it *all* got worse.

He stomped through the wet vegetation in the direction of Presley's barking.

The rain, together with the sweeping breezes, made him shiver worse than before. His clothes were soaking wet, and every step he took made mud splash under his boots. The forest floor was filled with bleached leaves, curved twigs, and everything else that belonged to Alaska's nature at this time of year.

But no traces to follow.

What are you expecting? Road signs and tracking maps?

Tom searched with the flashlight all around himself. These voices, where did they come from? They must come to him from somewhere else.

Signals.

He couldn't prevent any of it. He squeezed his hands against his ears. "Leave me alone!"

They silenced.

Tom continued walking.The beam illuminated the rain in the air, making it reflect like flying silver coins.

Another bark sounded straight ahead of him. He increased his pace and went through pine-needle filled puddles, past an eternity tree, and even past some wet seed grass blowing in the wind. The bark revealed he had to be close. But how close? Even though every step he took tore at his muscles and his head still banged with waves of pain, nothing would slow him down now.

You won't find anything, trucker!

Tom gritted his teeth. "Leave me alone!"

The dog barked again. This time to his left. Tom twisted in its direction but almost lost his balance. It wasn't possible. How could the dogs barks change direction like that?

"Presley?" His throat squeezed. Tom turned around again, and the fog surrounded him as if he had walked into a large cloud of smoke filled with rain. His lungs burned with every breath he took. Sweat ran down his face along with a bitter taste of salt and iron. Blades of grass sliced at his legs like long tongues. The trees swung toward him, whispering a deep and threatening language. It was like the whole forest stalked his footsteps.

Tom pointed the flashlight to the side. It illuminated the blown trees that lay on the ground among the grassy patches. In some places the soil was damp while in other places it was impossible to get through at all. Moss-covered stones penetrated the dirt like rotting tombstones. The wind whistled between the trees with a child's whisper. The shattering rain filled Tom's ears with a steady rumbling. But another sound also appeared out there. This time it wasn't a bark. This time it was something *else*. Something rough, like scratching claws on tree trucks.

Tom's heart thumped.

What scares you, trucker?

A cold breeze rushed past him, like the breeze from a wide-open window, and something followed it; a merciless shadow, filled with the secrets of the forest.

Whatever way Tom turned, everything looked the same. A slow tense of panic grabbed him as his throat tightened, until a raw wind reminded him to keep going. He skipped a couple of smaller bushes and leafy ferns, continued over some tricky undergrowth, but still couldn't find the dog anywhere. Some parts of the forest consisted of uneven and angular terrain with moss-covered rocks, low-growing grass, and crooked plants and trees standing apart from each other. Other parts of the forest were impenetrable with overgrowth. Among its long, sturdy grass blades and coniferous trees, curved plants with tines hung like menacing thorns. The dark shadows filled pieces of the forest, threatening with the worst possible secrets and inexplicable mysteries the world had yet to see.

Tom spun in circles. "Presley? Buddy? Where the hell are you?"

Nature had captured Tom in its talons and slowly squeezed the air out of him. Deep in his bones the panic of flight sharpened like a blade of cold steel. His stomach sank and sweat dripped from his scalp. He tensed his shivering body, flashlight in hand, and staggered forward until he tripped and lost his balance on a dead tree trunk covered with mushrooms. The flashlight flew out of his hand, and a pain escalated from his left arm up to his shoulder. His feet slid in the mud as he tried getting up. He crawled against the flashlight, slid in the mud, and then grabbed it. He put the flashlight between his teeth and pulled himself up with the help of feral grass. As he righted himself, the unknown sound once again drilled through him with a wheezing shriek. The deeper he went into the forest, the more isolated the sound became, as if it came from somewhere *below* him, deep down from the underworld, calling to him.

He turned around and scratched his knees against a mossy stone. "Presley!" he shouted. "Where the hell are you?"

Why don't you turn around, Tom?

Tom pressed his hands to his ears and tried to shut out the voices. "Please," he whispered. "Go away!"

And they did, but instead, another sound from behind almost made him lift from the ground.

CHAPTER

13

IT WAS THE SOUND of an overturning tree that scared him. Tom tried to grab a hold of a hanging twig nearby, but fell backwards and slammed his ass in a group of moss filled branches.

It took a couple of seconds before he directed the shaking flashlight to the overturned tree on the ground. With his heart in the throat, and his pulse bouncing inside him like a road drill, he swore to himself, then to nature and finally to the rain, for messing with him.

Scared, trucker?

He grabbed a hold of a bush and didn't react when it cut him on the arms. He pulled himself up, and staggered away in an unknown direction.

The moist stink of spruce bark and rotting leaves, mixed with the aroma of wet moss, penetrated around him. He continued walking, continued struggling, until he stopped by a couple of fuzzy, green stones bigger than him, to catch his breath. The rain continued to pelt him. But the stones next to him stood angled against each other next to an even larger rock, like a reversed V. His shaking body pulsed into sharp tenses. How far could he continue out there? If he wanted to survive, he had no other choice than to seek cover under the rock formation. Any protection would be a good protection. If the animals didn't kill him out here, the weather would.

Don't let the animals get you!

Tom bent down on his knees and aimed the flashlight into the opening. If he didn't want to freeze to death, the stones would, at least, keep the rain from hastening his journey to hypothermia. But he couldn't give up searching for Presley, could he? He aimed the flashlight back into the infinite forest, and his eyes were filled with tears.

"I'm so sorry, buddy," he whispered, and doubtfully edged his way in under the rock formation. He angled the flashlight against the wet ground, which was filled with wilted leaves, cones, and seeds. Insects wriggled and squiggled along the dirt as if the rainwater were a poison to them all. From the inside of the forest, it was well-nigh impossible to observe the sky above. The darkness had come quick and without any warning. Even if someone was searching for Tom right now from above, would they even notice him down there? He would be a coniferous in an anthill. Perhaps he had to make himself visible somehow, but it would be risky—a risk he wasn't willing to take right now. Who could he trust?

He leaned, half lying with his back against one of the stones, and tried to take a deep breath. The rock chopped at his back, but it *had* to work for the moment. His body had become so heavy and unwieldy, and his eyelids were heavy. Every movement made his muscles cramp. Even if his body needed rest, his mind still told him to get out and search for Presley.

With his head leaned back against the cold surface, he couldn't help but cry with a loud and hacking voice. Why did he deserve to be under protection while his dog ran around out there in the forest all alone? It wasn't fair, but Tom Richards had learned years ago, life wasn't fair, not anywhere in the world.

He closed his eyes and tried to determine how long they've been out in the forest. How long since the crash? Hours? Days? He couldn't remember. It was all a blurry steam inside him. He chewed the insides of his cheeks in frustration. Under the stones, he remained a helpless man. But outside the stones, he would be equally helpless. He hadn't been able to save Presley from the forest yet, but he couldn't give up trying. It would be suicide to go out again during the night to search. The darkness didn't only suffocate him from the outside but from the inside as well. And there were many hours left until there would be any sort of daylight in the sky again—if daylight ever came. Maybe the world had stopped rotating, and Tom had reached a spot of endless shadows, a place where the sun didn't rise again until pure justice reigned.

His body shook.

The world was no longer a secured place. It *never* had been. It had fooled everyone with its superficial veil, but not Tom, not anymore. He clenched his fists and pushed them against his teeth.

See what you've done, trucker! Satisfied?

Tom hit his fist in the wet ground, almost breaking the flashlight. He gasped for his breath and widened his eyes. He had to be careful; if he didn't have the flashlight by his side, the darkness would permeate the forest, making it impossible to perceive anything from under the stones. He would be a victim for everything, even the overgrown wilderness with its dangerous terrain. But even with the flashlight, he still didn't stand a chance out there. And he had to be conservative with the batteries. He couldn't leave the flashlight on overnight. The glow from it already seemed weak. He had no choice but to extinguish the beam and cover himself with darkness until daylight. The idea made his stomach turn.

One, two, three.

Breath.

Tom twisted the flashlight, and the glow died out. The first few seconds, it made his breath short out, and he couldn't get any air at all. It was like his lungs stopped, and he had to struggle to not get panicked. The darkness, the mysterious darkness, the *endless* darkness choked him. It slithered through him the same way it always had; it gnawed on him from the inside. If he wanted to break the panic, he had to find something else to focus on.

A dull glow from the moonlight reflected in golden hues on the stones outside and threw shadows of the curly moss. On the tree peaks, a tint of brownish copper appeared.

He had to stare. Stare until he couldn't anymore.

And he did.

During the night, the rain came and went while bubbling clouds swept past the area. Tom had to keep it together and stay strong. Not only for Presley. For Margaret too.

Birds came from time to time and swept across the canopy of trees above him. Their wings rustled the leaves on the spiny branches. Overhead, the gray-colored moon now stepped forward, and the clouds moved apart. In the shelter of the thickened trees, the night hours were long.

The temperature dropped.

Tom trembled. Why didn't he wear more clothes? Why didn't he take that ugly raincoat before heading out into the forest? He pushed his hands against his head and pulled his hair in all directions. It had all been a mistake. He was a mistake. And everything he did was a mistake. The biggest mistake was to take on the damn job to begin with. What had he been thinking?

Now he was lost, without Presley, and couldn't do anything.

You're worthless, trucker.

Tom Richards hit his head with his fists.

One, two, three, four ... fucking *five.*

Counting isn't going to help you this time!

Tom laughed a brief one before hitting himself once more in the head. Wasn't life somewhat of a joke? As he sat there with only a flashlight, a cigarette package in his chest pocket, and a lighter by his side, the world continued to rotate as if nothing had happened. He didn't even have his keys anymore. He must have dropped them somewhere on the road. Or in the forest. Or in the damn truck. But it didn't matter anymore. The only thing mattered was his dog.

He laughed a soundless laugh that bubbled out of him like a too long receipt from the receipt machine at the store, where an annoyed cashier sighs for each new item.

Is this everything for today, sir? If so, your total comes to $921.85. How will you be paying today? With cash or with your own life? And would you like your receipt pressed down in your throat, sir?

When he was finished laughing, he continued staring out against the rainy darkness. What the hell had he been thinking? He was alone out there, alone without anyone knowing. It had all been a mistake. And Margaret, what was she doing now? Perhaps she had just gotten out of a hot shower and was sitting with her mother in front of the television, drinking some tea, completely unaware of what had happened. If Tom never got home again, would she ever find out what had happened to him? Would *anyone* ever find out? His hope wavered with the wind. He couldn't stand the thought of himself dying for nothing. To sit in the darkness without being able to do anything at all but wait, made him shake, not only from the cold, but from the frustration brought with it.

Who put you out there, trucker? You did it all by yourself, yes, you did!

A painful force went through him together with another voice, and his eyes blurred again.

"Quiet," he whispered, and pressed his hands tighter against his skull and tried to squeeze out the ache. Nothing happened. Like if the voices were lodged deep in his skull.

Again, he clenched his fist and hit himself in the head.

Woho, continue, captain! Is that all you have? One more, captain! Come on! Show me-

Another hit, this time right in the forehead.

He cried again, soundless, while glancing around by the dark stones. How long would he have to stay under there? If the rain didn't stop, he had to get out there, even if he died trying. But September month could be cold, making it an early winter. How long *could* he stay there, before he died? Once, he had heard about a Norwegian truck driver who had become stuck in his truck during a harsh winter in Oslo in the late 90s. It happened during a heavy snowstorm. The truck's battery froze, and the driver had been forced to cut off the upholstery from the seats in order to stay warm. One week later, when the snowstorm had calmed down, the police found his truck. After they had dug him out, the man showed clear signs he had lost his mind. He had eaten all his toes on his right foot to silence his hunger, ready to taste the leg. But he had kept warm, at least.

Tom threw a gaze at his boots. He was hungry, but not *that* hungry.

Yet.

He forced his eyes shut. He *had* to sleep. But could he? He hadn't slept in more than a day. Perhaps two? He couldn't remember. What could he remember? His thoughts were like a pancake batter; the ingredients were there, but not in place.

Tom opened his eyes and stared into the inky blackness. The rain continued to spit at him. His neck tightened with sharp pain lacing up to the base of his skull. As a child, and later on as a teenager, he had been scared of the dark. It had destroyed much of his childhood, but when his friend showed up, he wasn't alone any longer. When Tom started high school, it had become easier not to think about it as he found new friends in a new environment under new conditions. More interests emerged; women attracted him with their curves, and he developed an ability he hadn't before been able to achieve. He could wake up at night, get up to pee and drink a glass of juice or soda, and then fall back into sleep without any worries. It could go a couple— almost up to three weeks—before the darkness reminded him it had the advantage. Sometimes, at night, his eyes got stuck in an empty murk, in a cramped room, on a closed street, or when the light had died out somewhere. He often found himself staring at nothing and forced himself to look away. Just like he now did. What tempted him? Nobody knew. Not his mother, or even Miss Paterson knew. But when he had met Margaret, his fear of darkness had vanished like a laundry stain. Her presence obliterated all sorts of domestic ideas and thoughts he earlier had devoted to the darkness. She converted the darkness into light for him creating peace. When he woke up and saw her beside him, a blanket of comfort settled over him. But would he ever do it again? She had always been his light.

Don't think about her, Tom! Because she doesn't think about you! Don't you get that?

"Shut up!" Tom raked his hand through his dripping hair and gasped for his breath. How could he have been so stupid fighting with Margaret all those years? Would he ever see her again? Would he ever smell her neck again, kiss her soft lips, and whisper in her ear the way he used to? Would he ever be able to make her eggs the way she wanted in the morning again, and squeeze her tight by him on the porch when a storm came? A tear rolled down his cheek. Several tears. Would he ever be able to look into her eyes again and tell her how much he loved her?

He had been a terrible husband these last couple of years. How could he have treated her the way he did, with all the name calling, sighs of annoyance, mocking, and other nastiness that damaged the relationship? He would do *everything* in his power to get her back, to hold her, and to kiss her. But he couldn't do anything now. He was lost, hurt, and left for the wildness to prey upon. And it was all his fault.

Tom glanced out against the foggy darkness, and the rain changed directions as the intrusive wind grew stronger. It howled in the air with a desperate scream. It rustled somewhere in the beauties of nature, and a creaking, whispering rode in with the gusts. It could have been an air pocket that created the sound, but it sounded so made up, almost as an unclear mimic.

No.

Tom forced his eyes shut again. He had to sleep now. Had to gain some energy in order to survive.

When his mind decided to take a break, he slept—dreamless.

And when the fog disappeared, a dark twilight crept in with its damp wraith.

CHAPTER

14

TOM WOKE UP AND strained his neck when his chin fell forward against his chest. He opened his eyes, and the darkness surrounded him like before, but the rain no longer hit with the same power. It had, instead, decreased to a thin drizzle. But the cold, humid air made him curl up like a child in the womb. The sallow light from the moon continued farther into the dark and unknown forest and lit up some bigger trees a few feet away. On a branch close by sat a pair of ravens crouched together. They wheezed out their discords towards the world's secret valleys as if they ruled the night with their mysterious presence. In their world, perhaps, they did, but things were different here.

How long had he been sleeping? He could no longer unfurl his fingers away from his hard-knitted hands, and it could mean hours. In the daylight, his hands would have been colorless, on the border of blue, but as not much could be seen in the dark, he concluded that he was in bad shape but would be alright. There was no point in turning on the flashlight. He didn't want to risk wasting more battery power. Not if it wasn't necessary.

Tom took a deep breath. His heartbeat pounded with a slow thrum, and the pulsing in his head radiated throughout his body. His feet had the same stiff coldness as his fingers. He tried to wiggle them. It stung. Instead, he lifted up his legs and bit his lower lip as he frowned. The attached muscles from his legs to his back shook. Most of his blood had diverted to his organs to provide protection. The chill made his teeth chatter. How much more could he stand?

He grimaced. Mustering all the strength he had left, he pulled his boots out of the mud in an attempt to keep the remaining warmth. They slid a bit on the ground, but he managed to get into a fetal position. His fingertips and toes now thumped in an angry rhythm that pulsated up and down through his limbs. His breath appeared like a miniature smoke cloud in front of him. Would someone be able to see it? Perhaps. If not humans, there must be animals that both saw and heard in the darkness well enough to spot him. How good was the security under those stones?

Tom crossed his arms and shoved his hands down under the shirt, right into the sweaty armpits. His armpits still had the heat he was looking for. His fingers pricked and stuck as the blood flowed back through them. He tried to take a deep breath, but his lungs filled with frigid air, which made him cough. He had to stay quiet, but how could he?

You can't! They will hear you, and when they do, they will get you!

Tom shook his head. No. He had to make a fire before he froze to death. It might be his only way to survive, and it would scare away any predators. Or would it lure them to him instead? He couldn't think straight. He had the lighter in his chest pocket, but where would he get any dry firewood out there? Going out now in the forest, in search of firewood, wouldn't only be dangerous, but he'd also risk getting lost and not finding his way back to the stones. He had nothing to protect himself with. It would be a dangerous mission. Something he couldn't afford.

An owl landed somewhere close to the boulders. It howled into the night as if reporting to the rest of the animals what happened on the other side of Dalton Highway.

Without any warning, the rain came back with fierce vengeance.

Tom sighed.

He couldn't do anything more than wait.

Wait for what? To die, tough trucker? To let your dog die?

Tom closed his eyes. "Shut up," he whispered. "No more. Shut up. I don't wanna hear more."

But you have to listen, trucker! Listen to nature. What do you hear?

Tom swallowed. All kinds of noises played together out there in the wild; twigs broke as cones fell with the swaying of the tree branches. The leaves landed with a light tenderness around him. Some foxes sneaked around among the snares and yipped, their shrieks shrill like frightened children's cries. The agonizing screams of whistling winds carried more sounds to his ears; the rain on the trees appeared like distant whip cracks, like snapping fingers. On the ground, the sound dulled into small shoes running on fine cotton mats, like those red carpets in the hotel corridors. Sporadic breezes caused the tree leaves to shake like wet cats. Near the ground the wind swirled with a silent yowl, far from the howling scream that shook the bushes. The grassy areas swayed as if a rattlesnake slid through them. When the wind drifted past smaller passages filled with broken rocks, it whispered secrets and lies. And something else also came with the wind. A humming noise. It penetrated throughout the forest, like the loud purr from a low playing violin, striking a gentle tone that requires conscious listening.

Tom opened his eyes and glanced at the golden reflections beyond the rocks. He swallowed again, but his mouth had become dry. A thought of drinking from the ground in front of him made him nauseous. He closed his eyes again and clenched his teeth.

Despite its distance, the noise morphed into a heavier rumbling tone, like a machine moving faster and faster, higher and higher, so ... *close.*

Tom widened his eyes into the darkness. He couldn't take his eyes off. It was as if an unseen power forced his sight there, with a child's curiosity. The endless, black, September night stared back at him with merciless emptiness, but yet full of hidden surprises.

In that moment, somewhere in the dark, a movement approached with a heavy force through the trees. Almost as if the wind couldn't be stopped.

Tom's stomach sank like a stone in water.

And the sound from the dark came closer.

Tom held his breath. He laid still, with the thought that no would ever hear him scream if he did.

The sound came again, but now it seemed dull, dark, and isolated, throbbing somewhere around him like a sluggish knock on an old hardwood gate.

Thunk thunk thunk.

Tom's eyes watered. He had an involuntary force to empty his bladder as if his life hung on it. With stiff fingers, he pulled out his right hand from his left armpit and yanked down the zipper on his pants. The metal of the zipper stung in his fingers. But he had no other choice. He refused to piss his pants.

He took out his cold and shrunken penis and let out the hot liquid next to him. The urine flowed beneath him as the smell penetrated the air with a smoke cloud. The ground beneath him seemed denser, closer, with more intensity—as if—he had brought it to life.

He stuffed his penis back into his shorts without breathing. He couldn't help but stare back into the dark void as if it was trying to tell him something.

Scared, trucker?

Without thinking, he gripped the flashlight and squeezed the handle to warm it up.

The moonlight only illuminated a few spots in the forest. The tree tops consisted of the same golden color as before, but now with a dark glint around them.

Once again, a hard clap came up through the ground. An underground crashing.

Tom winced. His heart now rushed in the chest, and his pulse bounced in his ears. His blood pressure rose in soaring waves. He searched for every possible change out there, tried to catch every movement, shadow, or sign that revealed itself. His instincts told him to run as fast as he could, but his body could no longer move. The blood drain from his face as his body stung like thousands of ground-dwelling wasps were attacking him.

And *something* swept past the trees in front of him, making a hollow swoosh. Threatening shadows scurried across the pale, moonlit tree trunks, right through the cold September night.

Tom squeezed the flashlight tighter, and in the same moment, white flying orbs appeared in front of his eyes, penetrating the forest. They moved back and forth, up and down along the trees as if searching for something.

With each breath, Tom's lungs joined together in a tight wave. Warm sweat ran down his chilled skin, pulsing like hammering nails into flesh. The stones shielded him from the outside, yet he was trapped inside there.

A growling rode on the wind, and the white, circulating orbs grew larger by the trees.

They came closer.

He held his breath.

Closer.

Tom lit the flashlight, and in front of him, something dark and hairy emerged from the darkness. All thoughts of survival disappeared with a sudden internal detonation. Somewhere inside, he should have known already. It should have been in there somewhere, like a calculated phenomenon of the rise of life, but it had tricked him and lured him into the corner of the darkness.

A creature in front of him walked on all fours, and its body leaned forward with a loping rhythm. It wrenched its massive, shaggy head against the ground and came right against him.

CHAPTER

15

TOM TURNED OFF THE light in the same moment as he lit it.

He struggled not to faint from the sight of what came against him. There could only be one creature in Alaska with that kind of size and movement. As a child, his father had taught him everything about bears.

Tom shook. Vibrations shot through his clenched muscles and demanded he flee. One part of him had already fled in his mind, far away through the forest towards the limits of safety. In reality he couldn't move an inch. In reality he was caught.

He struggled to hold his breath, but he couldn't last for long. His lungs made a low, howling noise with each breath he had to take. But he needed to be quiet. Couldn't afford to reveal himself inside there. If the bear was hungry, Tom could end up as a meal. The thought roiled his insides. His father had taught him how the animal's teeth could tear through a human's flesh and bones without any difficulties, something he never forgot.

No, no.

He didn't want to get chewed on. Not now, not today, not *ever*.

He lowered his gaze to his arms and forced himself to take a deep breath. No matter what, he had to stay focused. But the sight of his arms made his eyes widened even more. Both his arms and hands were covered in small, bloody cuts. What if the bear picked up the scent of his blood? He was now left to the wilderness' macabre processes. And Tom didn't stand a chance if the animal attacked.

The bear came closer.

Tom made himself smaller. The bulletin board at the rest area flashed in his memory. All the pictures of the missing people came in ambiguous flashbacks. Had the bears taken them? Had *this* bear taken them? Was he next in line?

In terrifying slow motion, the bear rose onto its back legs in front of the rock formations. It wrinkled its nose with a slight snorting. Its sense of smell outweighed its eyesight.

Tom squeezed the flashlight in his hand. Even if the thought was absurd, it was his only weapon. If the bear decided to come at him, the flashlight would *have* to protect him, at any cost. But it wouldn't cause much damage.

It won't do anything!

The bear continued sniffing, now against the rock formations.

Tom tightened his muscles, and couldn't breathe. He had to get away from there. But to panic, shout, or even run away, would only create more problems. Bigger problems. A human's temporary outbursts of mind could make any animal furious.

The bear growled with a low tone.

Tom's sweat turned into a sticky layer on his skin. He closed his eyes and tried to refocus, but the panic imploded inside him. He had to get away from there, now.

The growling continued, now a bit higher.

Tom gritted his teeth and peeked around on the ground after *something*. But he needed a big weapon. A *stronger* weapon. A more dangerous weapon. Something longer and sharper: something that could hurt the bear bad if he had to. But nothing more than twigs, pebbles, and pinecones belonged around him.

What are you waiting for, trucker?

The flashlight shook in his hand.

The bear wasn't more than a couple of feet away from him now, sniffing.

Tom had to do *something*. But what? His nerves were about to break and his pulses to implode.

A howling sound made the bear back on all fours, before it moved towards the east with a rapidity. The bear rocked back and forth, continuing to search the ground. It panted as if it was tired and needed to find food in a hurry. And in the next second, it was gone, swallowed by the darkness.

Tom tried to breath. His chest rattled. Pulses in his body bounced from everywhere. Could the bear really be gone? Where? The sound had made it haste its way away from there. But *where*? He had to focus, and keep an eye open. There were plenty of different species around Alaska: the grizzly bear, the black bear, the kodiak bear, and even the polar bear. Anyone with any sense didn't want to be close to any bear under any circumstances. Even a bear in chains could be dangerous. Even though the bear wasn't the size of either a kodiak or a polar, it still had the same massive, sharp teeth. Although they were omnivorous animals, that for most parts ate berries and plants, it sometimes happened that livestock came along in their meals. Bears did, after all, have bad eyesight. An advantage for Tom. At least for now. It could be the only advantage he would ever have against it. But most bears didn't approach humans on purpose, but nobody wanted to stumble over any hollow tree trunk in which a bear lay or fall, uninvited, into a bear cave. It would be certain suicide. But Tom's father had taught him early how important it was to stay calm if you met a bear. Bears could become an instant threat if they turned out to be injured or had cubs nearby. Tom had to protect himself. Without a real weapon, or even bear spray by his side, he was screwed. What he needed was something dangerous. A sharp twig, perhaps. A *long* and sharp twig.

Tom took a deep breath, and the sour smell of wet moss penetrated his nostrils. But the danger wasn't over. The bear could be anywhere around, but he couldn't wait any longer. He had to get away from there while he still could, while he still had any legs to run with.

Tom crawled out from the stones, and shoved himself to standing with the help of the stone. He glanced around through the darkness, but it wasn't until he lit his flashlight again in search for a weapon, as the sight made his heart to freeze.

This time, the bear came bounding right toward him.

All the talk and instructions on how to stay calm and sensible during such an occasion, now disappeared in an explosion of white, silky silence. Tom's face paled like high tide on a beach. All sounds evaporated, and the world stopped spinning.

He had only two choices left.

Flee or fight.

CHAPTER 16

IF TOM EVER WANTED to see his dog again, he had to swallow all fright and run until his legs gave out. The rock formations wouldn't save him this time.

He ran through the gushing rain. The light from the flashlight dangled in the darkness. The unknown shapes of the wilderness threatened him from all angles—and a beast was after him. He had to flee from the bear before it caught him. Before he became part of the fateful nature of dark secrets. The forest around him did have a long and almost barren area with low-growing grass. But one misstep could mean a huge failure; he could end up in an overgrown net of vegetation like a spider's prey.

His lungs were on fire.

Pine branches scratched his stiff, cold cheeks. He whimpered with pain and crouched down under a fir tree laced with cobwebs. The threads stuck to his mouth and arms. A twig snagged his hair and yanked away his cap. He tried to dodge the branch, but his head was jerked back by its claw-like limbs. Rain splattered his eyes. He grabbed the twig with shaky hands, snapping it in half. Part remained in his hair as he continued onward.

Tom crossed some leafy brush, legs heavy, and pushed himself onward through the short, wild grass. He could get caught in a jumble of rocks or tangle of branches. It didn't matter. He had to get away from there.

Tom ran past some shady barked trees, until he reached a steep hill. The darkness spilled down its slope; it was his greatest chance of survival. Bears didn't like to run down slopes. Or was it a myth? It didn't matter either.

He had to move, now.

A growling appeared from behind, together with the sound of breaking twigs.

Tom rushed down the slope with his boots skidding against the wet undergrowth. He tried to maintain his balance, but the rain made the ground too slick. He slipped, landing on his back with a thump. His breathing disappeared for a moment, and the trees flickered past him as he slid downward. He hit a patch of green, filled with grass and Sitka spruces. The long blades spread like tentacles around him, as if trying to grab onto legs.

It's coming for you!

Another sound from somewhere behind. This time, a dark and long-spun growling.

The bear was close.

Tom gripped the top of a cracked tree trunk and pulled himself up with a gasp. The bark scratched his already sore hands into a burning mess. He turned back to the slope with his eyes wide open. No bear in sight.

Yet.

Wherever the bear was, Tom *needed* to get away from here.

He pushed himself forward, but his foot sank into some wet moss. Deep mud enveloped his boot and sucked him in. He tried to twist his foot backward, but nothing happened. He tried to yank his foot upward with all his strength, but whatever sucked him down in the mud, now pulled him deeper. A rush of panic caused him to yank at the stuck boot. His nerves were about to break out from his body. The rain spat at him, and the wind tore him in different directions. A ringing of vibrations moved closer into his ears. He was immobilized, like an animal in a trap, and somewhere behind came the snapping sound of more breaking twigs.

This was it. The bear would come bounding down the slope anytime now. It would jump on him, and knock him down into the muddy wetland. Shake him with such violence that the last noises Tom would hear would be the snapping of his own neck. Sound was, after all, the last working sense before death took over. And then the bear would eat him alive.

Prepare to be bear food, trucker!

Tom fell down, ass first, and all the cells in his muscles vibrated with terror. He put the flashlight in his mouth and grabbed whatever vegetation sprang from the ground. He got a hold of the long tentacle-like grass and tore himself backwards. The shoots snapped through his hands. He gasped in pain. A pulsing signal of fatigue sizzled through his body.

Another dark grunt sounded from behind, together with some rapid, heavy, wet throbbing.

Tom crawled backwards on his elbows through the mud. It was like his foot was caught in a slimy jam that wanted to dissolve him alive.

A bush next to him rattled. His heartbeat almost knocked him back over. A small Cedar Waxwing bird appeared from the bush and flew over him. It had a collection of bulrush in its beak. The bird drew Tom's attention to a dangling branch above him. The cold made his joints lock up on him. It was him versus nature. But he still had a chance.

You'll never get out of here alive!

Tom gripped the branch as another intense pain tore from his hand all away through his arm. But he couldn't stop now. He continued to pull with all his remaining strength and managed to raise himself upward, half standing, as his arms pulsed with dull thumps.

A short, splintering noise appeared from behind, like the sound of a snapping tree trunk, and something in Tom exploded.

This was the moment where everything would fall to pieces. This was the moment he would die. But he couldn't turn around now. Couldn't face the danger. Couldn't face death.

But with the last of his efforts, he tensed his arms and threw his body weight from side to side. With a sopping sound, his boot shot up from the mud like a plunger getting pulled up in a toilet. He managed to scramble to his feet. He jumped across the moss to the left, and sprinted deeper into the forest.

A heavy force made the mud splash.

The bear was right behind him.

It's coming!

The lactic acid pumped through Tom's legs, as if they consisted of red-hot tendons. The darkness obscured everything in its path. The light from the flashlight went from side to side. The light revealed everything around. Everything except slight gray figures of nature's creation—and the sound of stomping *paws*.

A rush penetrated the thick tree tops with a whistle. Tom's chest rose and fell like a rocking ship. The wet air shot through him like arrows. The inside of his throat had become sticky. He couldn't regain any breath at all. He had nowhere to flee. But he still continued onward, jumped over a fallen tree trunk, when everything disappeared in a hundredth of a second. His left foot hit the edge of a moss-covered stone and he fell straight to the ground. The flashlight flew out of his hand, and the light rolled away in the grass. He caught himself with his sore palms. Pine cones, twigs, and stone remains all twisted into his flesh, digging in deep.

Tom twisted around, gasping for his breath, and the bear emerged from the darkness a few feet away from him.

A breeze of horror brought his whole world to a halt.

Tom swallowed his Adam's apple and puked it up in the same moment. His body surged with an acrobatic burst of fright. Escape. Fight. *Anything.* The panic rushed through him like the metallic sound of a train on a rail.

An inner force made him roll aside, where he grabbed the nearest twig he could find. He raised it like an African bush hunter with a poisoned wooden spear.

The bear came at him, grunting and panting.

In the gloomy, black air, their gaze met in a desperate hurry—Tom's wide-open, horrified eyes against the bear's vague, black, eager stare.

Tom's heart was about to explode. He summoned all his strength and aimed at the nose. But, like a car swerving off the road, the bear took another turn. It ran by Tom, leaving him alone with a look of awe on his face. The sound vibrated through the ground right next to him, and the bear's clumsy steps faded away.

Tom turned. His whole body was trembling. The bear had vanished into the darkness. Had it missed him? No, they had *made* eye contact. It couldn't have missed him. It wasn't possible. Something *else* had happened. But what?

Tom closed his eyes and gasped for breath. The unknown growled like an inner anxiety, as if it came from supernatural impulses where intuitions and warnings from the sixth sense tumbled through the spherical forest.

An idea struck him, that maybe the bear was never after him.

Maybe it was fleeing from something.

CHAPTER

17

THE FOREST HAD A history, and that history was dangerous. For Tom Richards, his life had now become a struggle between life and death, but the worst had not yet come.

He shuddered between the trees, like a leaf caught in the wind, and it would take a while before the shock from running from a bear lay down.

The temperature continued to sink with the approaching night. But the rain still made everything worse with its relentless downpour.

Tom had escaped a beast, but Presley was still out there somewhere. But under the prevailing circumstances it became more difficult to do something about it when the weather fought anyone who might try. Tom couldn't even make a fire as long as the rain kept on the way it did. The water would fizzle out any attempts at a successful flame. But he still needed some kind of protection, a roof over his head, a weapon, *something* that could help him out along the search. The rock formation was gone. He couldn't return. But it was too risky. Once, he had planned on buying bear spray. Some kind of bear insurance was needed for anyone who lived in Alaska, but like much else in his life, it never happened. He could've brought the spray in the truck with him, even if he never ended up using it. But no. He couldn't even accomplish that little task.

You're a worthless man, Tom Richards! Don't you get that?

Tom needed some kind of protection, but he neither had the knowledge nor the time to build a wind break or shelter. In reality, it wouldn't come off as easy as the survivors on the Discovery channel made it look. He had to do whatever it would take to stay alive, but only if it would give him Presley back. Without the dog, he wouldn't leave the forest alive. But still, there was some kind of danger out there that had scared away a grown bear, and whatever it was, it was lethal—if nothing stopped it.

Tom had to find the dog. But he was now far away from the truck, the only protection he once had, with food and water. He pulled his shaking hand through his dripping wet hair and sighed. How could he have been so stupid losing control of the truck? What had made him do it? Everything that had happened was his own fault. If he wouldn't have lost the control of the damn truck, Presley would be safe by now. They would *both* be safe. He *needed* to find him. He would do anything for the dog. Presley was the child he and Margaret never had. The child they had been trying to get for years, which, in time, had shattered them both when it had all failed. They had tried for a long time after they got married, without any success. Presley had become their unknown savior. Already, from the start, where a scheduled visit to the doctor had shown a suspicion of a normal lapse in ovulation, it had become a warning sign for them both. It happened to all women once or more during their menstrual cycles, the doctor had explained to her. Margaret had agreed with it, of course, but when the months drug on and the pregnancy tests continued to show the same bleak results, it meant more doctor visits. More money. More *work*. The responsible, foreign-born doctor, Fredriech, suspected Margaret could have had cysts or some underdeveloped ovaries, which could give rise to hormone disorders, but nothing really proved it. Margaret had to do an ovulation test and use a fertility monitor, which neither showed anything wrong or even any failures that her luteal phase was too short. On paper, everything looked good, but in practice, it all fell against the ground. Doctor Fredriech suspected Margaret might have early onset menopause, something that could make a woman in her late twenties explode in tears.

Dr. Fredriech explained it was rare, but it sometimes happened to women even younger than Margaret. "A matter of fact. Incomprehensible change of life. Have you two ever thought about adop-tion?" He said it with a pause between *adop* and *tion*. But they hadn't thought about it, so Fredriech continued to run tests for possible blockages in the fallopian tubes, some growth in the uterus, Chlamydia, all the levels in Margaret's blood. He studied her cycle and couldn't discover anything out of the ordinary. Margaret neither drank alcohol by then, smoked, used drugs, or anything else that could knock her body off balance. She was a caring woman who neither stressed, nor took Tylenol when she had a headache. She believed in the wonders of nature. If she had been so good all the time, the cards could only fall in another direction.

Even if he had suspected it from the start, Tom had never asked for any tests on himself. The years passed, and having children became an impossible mission. When Margaret had turned thirty, they didn't even talk about it anymore, and although both of them knew it wasn't worthwhile to continue, they still had that desire to keep something alive. They had, on one occasion, considered adoption, perhaps even going to another country to give a foreign-born child a good chance in life. The desire had disappeared with time.

They dealt with the disappointment in different ways; Margaret went down in the wine cellar (although, she sometimes said she cleaned the shelves, even though she came up and smelled of alcohol), and Tom spent his time drinking beer out in the barn while he fixed the pickup on days he didn't have a job to care about, which didn't happen too often.

One day that all changed: a picture in the local news had shown a couple of German Shepherd puppies. They lived on a farm a couple of hours away. Tom had first shown Margaret the picture in the newspaper for fun but had considered it for real in the garage. Why not? A child seemed to be out of reach. An adoption would still not give them the biological consolation they were looking for. A puppy could be what they *needed*, for their own love and their relationship. Not long after, they went to see the dogs, and one of them was the big hunk o'love. So they bought it, named it Presley, and it became the child they couldn't have. But now, that dog, their *child*, had disappeared into the forest. And it was because of Tom.

You selfish idiot! Why are you such a stupid trucker? You're nothing but a stupid man, Tom Richards. An imbecile!

Tom squeezed his hands against his ears, but the voices continued.

You're a worthless trucker, who can't even handle some permafrost along the road.

You're a worthless husband.

And a worthless dog owner.

"Stop!" Tom couldn't hold in his tears any longer. It was *his* own fault. *Everything* was his own fault. And he couldn't leave the dog out there all alone. He had to continue searching, even if it would be the last thing he ever did.

He got down, half sitting with his shaking elbows pressed against the ground, even though his lungs were like violin strings close to breaking. But all he needed to think about was how to find his dog.

The light from the flashlight blinked, and the light weakened.

Tom glanced against the pearly looking clouds, and the night's darkness grew colder around him.

And something was still out there in the darkness, something sinister.

18

TOM RICHARDS CONTINUED HIS search through the forest for Presley, while an icy wind pulled through the darkness of the night. The rain splashed down the Dalton Highway and every imaginable movement was to fear. But still, merciless powers hid somewhere around, and the light from the flashlight didn't reach far.

When a movement appeared close by, Tom froze, and was drawn back to the thoughts of the bear. But when the moonlight shone against the creatures back, it showed a caribou—a magnificent wild caribou that existed throughout the forests of Alaska. No bigger than a Great Dane but big enough to tackle Tom to the ground if it wanted, and kill him.

It didn't.

The shadows of nature's creatures spun in the moonlight, and the caribou leaned forward with his gaze pointing to the ground. It curved its neck and popped down its head in the untouched, wild-grown, long grass with a warming scent. The animal grunted like a pig and picked up berries from the ground.

Tom followed the animals' movement. He stood like a curious child with big eyes observing what happened in front of him. He smiled, and an almost innocent giggle slipped out of him.

The caribou must have been hungry. It stood so silent and merciful in the grass, yet full of nature's cruelty and merciless tricks for survival.

The wind grew stronger, and in the same moment, the caribou directed its gaze toward Tom. In the next second, it jumped in the air and fled into the dark forest as if it was never there.

A raven shrieked from above, in a shadow covered by trees, and the wind stopped.

Tom didn't move. It was like the whole forest fell asleep, and like punching an ON button, the voices came back.

Who are you trying to fool, Tom Richards?

You won't find him! Your dog is dead!

And you're next, trucker!

The rain made him shiver, but he continued. He needed to search for protection, but each step he took hammered a hat made of nails deeper into his head.

You're not fooling anyone, big trucker. You're stuck here, and you know it, too.

Together with the voices, the intensity of the night swelled around him, pulsing from the inside out. And a sharp, whistling sound sliced through him like a river current with sharpened edges.

Tom sought protection down against the ground with its seductive, dark silence. He pressed his body to the earth as if it would stop the sounds, but instead, the darkness engulfed him, and the sounds swarmed over him, forcing itself inside his flesh. He pushed his hands against his ears, but the noises still crawled inside him like thousands of angry bees.

In desperation, he crawled in the direction of the moonlit trees. The wet seeds, remnants of cones, thorny plants, and the whole surface of nature burned into his palms. His breathing was shallow and crisp, as if his lungs were filled with poison.

A hushed sound, like a pressing breeze, creaked through the openings of the trees. Whatever was happening out there, he had to get far away from it.

Hide, trucker. But don't let the bed bugs bite you in the darkness!

Tom crawled onward into the darkness as panic gripped at his skin. The long grass sliced at his face. The whole world was spinning, and he spun with it.

He tumbled into a group of tangled weeds and bushes, and they grabbed at him, pulling at him and twisting him with evil laughter. He strained and flailed, kicked and hit, until he freed himself. The noises surrounded him and made him pant as he continued crawling farther into the darkness until he bumped into a ripped tree. He couldn't continue crawling like that until the sunlight came. No. Instead, he backed up against the tree, rested his head against the bark, and clamped his hands over his ears.

Don't be afraid of the darkness, Tom - be frightened!

The noises overwhelmed him.

He had to force them away.

Tom hit himself in the head with the flashlight.

The light was dimmed.

One, two—

CHAPTER

19

TOM WOKE UP WITH a twitch. A big squawking raven stood on his chest, ready to tear out an eye or two. Tom twitched with a silent scream. The raven spread out its wings and attacked with its beak. Tom tore himself up and stumbled backwards. The raven fell against the ground, before it disappeared behind a group of bushes.

Tom searched protection against a hard, thick bark, which he likened to a heavy pillar of Roman architecture. But this wasn't any kind of temple or peristylium within the Etruscan or Roman borders; he took cover in the shadow of Sitka spruce. It must have been the spot he had reached the night before. The spot where he had—had done what? It was all a murky oblivion, as if he had intentionally repressed it.

He looked around. The ground around him consisted of Forget Me Not-flowers, and the scent of green filled the sweeping wind through the forest. The burning, yellow, galactic star stood far up in the sky and provided warmth to the entire field, while birds flew north with rattling wings and sang an unwritten melody. Everything around him possessed a pastoral beauty that only could be fulfilled through years of nature's natural cultivation. The wind whistled in harmony with the tree branches, which swayed as if they were moving in for a hug.

And the flashlight was also next to him. He grabbed it, twisted it, and a paltry light, almost invisible in the daytime, shone against him. At least it still worked.

For now.

For a second, Tom found himself in a divine state. But as reality slowly grabbed him back, he couldn't accept what was around him as anything else but misleading behavior, which was strengthened by nature's external laws. He couldn't let himself be tricked.

Presley was still out there in the wild somewhere, maybe even searching for Tom himself. Tom couldn't wait longer. He had to get out there directly.

He leaned forward in the soil. His body was stinging as pulsating vibrations shot throughout every one of his muscles. His neck radiated with a series of stiff cramps for each time he turned his head.

The wind pulled through his clothes as a reminder of what he had to do. He straightened up with the help of a spruce.

He turned and glanced in all directions. Where should he go? Where should he even begin to search?

The forest didn't seem to be the same in daylight as it did during the darkness. It was once an evil death trap, but still as an ordinary forest with natural sounds, a place where no dark forces should even have the urge to exist. But it did. Bigger parts of the forest stood like barren fields with nothing but ground cover. The stormy weather had left behind masses of leaves and branches strewn about. Sun-bleached grass covered the rest of the land, swaying in the breeze.

On the ground, near Tom, appeared small piles of soil not bigger than a grown man's foot. Some piles were closer to each other as if it had been an archeological dig of excavated graves. Some of the plants were in harsh conditions, deceased on the inside, but never having decayed, like a ghost in human shape.

How was he supposed to find Presley out there? The forest was enormous, and the dog could be anywhere. He swallowed hard.

In front of him, green moss covered the ground and sharp stones hid underneath. It would be risky to go that way. A damaged foot didn't appeal to him at all, and an injury would derail his search. It had been a miracle he hadn't become more injured in the crash. The best way to find the dog had to be from high up, like from a tree. Down on the ground, nothing could be seen. He had to find a place where he could get a better view. But from where? Climbing in a tree would also be risky.

Tom glanced around. The mountains surrounded the landscape around him. They stood like giant stone silhouettes in the daylight and showed no mercy to the forest below. Could he get to a mountain close by, without expending too much energy? With nothing to eat or drink in God knew how long, his energy levels stood at low. And it had been a long time ago since his body had been exposed to such physical force. His legs were stiff, and his back tensed in fatigue. But that was no reason to give up. If he ever wanted to find Presley and get home again, he would have to overlook all his needs for now. He had no other choices. He could choose to search by the trees for an eternity, or try the mountain view. If the view from the mountain didn't give any results, he would have to get back to the forest, a place which now gave him the creeps.

Although he used to love the forest, Margaret had always been the one who had spent her time outside in the forest next to their yard. Through the years, Tom had somehow avoided it, as if the trees pushed him back, or as if this moment had occurred to him earlier. But he couldn't avoid it longer.

He took a deep breath.

To the west, turf-covered bogs stretched far beyond open fields. The distanced stood quiet and devastating, a cursed land haunted by what lurked beneath, ready to grab anything that walked upon it. To the east, the sun's rays created life for both plants and animals. Flowers stretched out with a proud sweep from the soil, as trees swayed with a quiet and harmonious dance to the singing birds above. The marshmallow clouds hung fluffy white in the sky. Could it really be the same place?

Tom didn't hesitate before he followed a grass-filled, rugged terrain around berry bushes crawling over the ground in front of him. He stopped, bent down so his knees popped, and gathered a handful of glistening blackberries. He filled his mouth with all he could take. The berries gave off a rough and sour character, which made his taste buds jump for joy, but the content also contained a bitter powder. He spat the berries on the ground and grimaced like a child who refuses to eat his vegetables. Had he mistaken the fruit to be blackberries? Margaret had picked blackberries behind their house for years. Sometimes they ate them together with vanilla ice cream. Sometimes with milk. These tasted nothing like those. Could they be poisonous?

Tom's stomach rumbled. Without knowledge of what was safe to eat, he couldn't risk eating anything at all. The blackberries, or whatever they were, extended a long way into the forest. But he would rather starve than try those again. Nature had misled him, again.

Tom kicked the bush and spat on it. Its beauty was deceiving.

He stretched out his tongue and scraped off the remaining berries with his nails. He scraped until a taste of iron grew in his mouth.

Tom kicked the bush again, but this time the bush folded, and something appeared inside it.

He raised his eyebrows, pushed down his boot in the bush and split it in two. The sight made him pull back his boot in disgust. It was a dead animal in there. It could have been laying there for days or even weeks, but it wasn't completely devoured. By the naked and broken ribs crawled whirling flies and other various insects. Some fell from the carcass and crawled away from the decaying flesh.

An acidic odor joined what was left of the animal's rancid body. It must have been there through both the heat and cold, through the wet and the dry. Its skull had a deformed look with a sunken forehead, like it had been trampled. The lower jaw lay ripped off in the grass next to it and exposed a number of human-like teeth. From its empty eyeball sockets, white maggots crawled back and forth until losing their grip and falling into a collection on the ground.

Tom raised his sight at the berries. They were covered in those white maggots. Maggots that crawled and fell. His eyes widened as he pulled back. His stomach bubbled with acid, while cramps bunched up his abdominal muscles. The cramps made him double over as he tensed his back muscles and crouched, in an unsustainable position, against the bushes. The stomach acid burned his throat and made him pitch forward to his hands and knees. His tongue's muscles pushed backward against his throat, and searing liquid, mixed with what could have been yesterday's small dinner, sprayed from his mouth.

Yellow mucus hung from his mouth. He used his shirt sleeve to wipe it away.

Tom turned around, still in disguise, and in the same moment, a bark sounded from the distance.

He froze. "Presley?"

When another bark came, he started to run.

20

TOM CONTINUED RUNNING IN the same direction the barking had come from.

A lush measure of forest marsh covered the ground in front of him, together with a dry, fur-like substance.

He continued through the uneven terrain and farther through some overgrown flowers and thickets of sprawling branches. The winds threw different levels of air pressure. The clouds swept past the sun, and, from time to time, the shadows sent nature into obscurity.

His legs shook, and his back itched with sweat, but he couldn't stop now. Presley was close.

Another bark.

"Presley!" he shouted. "Presley, where are you?"

He continued running until he came to a slope.

Behind him, the forest was silhouetted with the sun's glowing, warm rays. He stood still for a moment and explored his possibilities. The wind swept past him with a vague smell of damp soil, beetle dung, and some kind of sweetness.

He glanced down at the ground in front of him again. The long grasses mocked him. But it wasn't more than grass. He couldn't wait longer; Tom pushed himself through it. Flying insects swarmed him each step he took. A spider climbed his neck. He killed it with his palm, and its blood spread out on his shirt.

After a few steps down, he slipped on some slick soil. Some scrub-covered rocks gave way beneath his feet, and he grabbed a cracked conifer, hugging it like a lover.

When the slope got steeper, he tried to slow his downward trajectory, but his foot stuck in an overgrown plant root, and he fell. He landed on his side, scratched all over his front. For a second, he was still as the pain pulsated from his hip all the way up to his shoulders. He caught his breath, bit his teeth together, stood up, and quickly brushed off the leaves he had added to his outfit. He looked around and panted, sweat dripping from his forehead. But beside him, in the slope, lay a narrow object covered by the soil.

Go on, trucker! What are you waiting for?

But Tom couldn't move. Ever since he was a kid, he had been terrified of snakes. Sometimes he had nightmares of how they came crawling in his bed at night and squeezed him to death while no one heard his silent screams.

Tom glanced around without moving. Not far away from him, on the ground, lay a long, rough branch. No snake would stand between him and Presley. If he had to kill it, he would do it without hesitation.

He gently put the flashlight between his teeth and took a deep breath. In the next second, he jumped over the grass and picked up the branch. He directed the branch against the snake, but hesitated. What if it was toxic? One bite from a toxic snake could kill or paralyze a man in seconds. He could jump over it, and then continue after Presley, but he didn't want a snake chasing him. But a snake in Alaska?

Tom glanced around again. He had to get to Presley before he forever lost him.

He raised the stick and struck the snake with a quick chop. The snake didn't react. Neither Tom's rustle in the grass, or his threatening lunge made it move. It just lay there, prepared for an attack. But it made no noise, not even a single hiss from its tongue.

Another bark.

"I'm coming, buddy! Stay where you are!" Tom stretched out the long stick and poked the snake with another quick chop, not hard but not too lightly either, a perfect shot, like a professional billiard player.

No reaction.

Tom went one step closer. The sweat ran down his forehead. His palms were wet. He squeezed the branch tighter and held his breath. "Fucking snake."

Another chop, this time a bit harder.

Still nothing.

Tom breathed out. He put the stick under the snake, ready to throw it away, when *something* made him doubt. It was something with the snake's skin. It had a transparent look, similar to the color of watered milk. Most snakes had a taut skin, filled with muscles, etched with patterns of different colors. Sometimes with red and brown patterns, or black with yellow lines, colors indicating danger status. But this one had no markings, no eyes, mouth, or even nostrils. It didn't even have a head. What the hell was it in front of him if not a snake?

Tom wiped his forehead with the back of his grimy hand. He swallowed hard. The only logical thing came to him as in a subconscious and recurrent dream.

Human intestines.

A wave of realization crashed through him; an unexplored, evil force demanded attention behind the ominously shaped trees. The discomfort that grew in his chest was like a piercing saw, and he flung the organ away in disgust.

Presley barked again, this time further away.

"Presley!" Tom shouted, and raced down the rest of the slope. He ducked under a tipped fir tree when something tickled his cheek. He wiped it away, but the material didn't release.

Tom glanced at his hand, and the sight made him gasp.

What he held between his fingers had a soft but strong fiber.

Human hair.

He tore off the hair on his hand with a grimace, when a void dug itself deeper into him, and beads of sweat penetrated the skin on his forehead. He staggered sideways; a dizziness grew inside him. Wet grass and the previous year's ground cover surrounded his feet. If it weren't for Presley, Tom could have become stuck there, but the dog's barks broke him out of an extraneous chock.

Tom gasped for breath, and continued against the sounds. "Where the hell are you? Stay, buddy!"

After passing a couple of downed fir trees, a dim density reached the mountains above as the light faded. Dark cumulonimbus clouds moved in from the west, hovering over the peaks, and the wind whistled through the trees and threw the cold air against nature's already dazed sphere. Nothing more than a few birds that sought their way home ahead of the darkening clouds.

Tom went farther into the overgrown thicket, tore himself further in, when he approached what could have been a cave entrance. The opening stood about six feet tall and three feet wide. Around the access point, the grass seemed darker than anywhere else. It couldn't be because of the whirling shadows distorted by the mountain's uneven surface and the swinging tree branches. The mutated grass spread like raven wings, and even the flowers next to the cave lay rotten on the ground in what appeared to be grey ashes.

In that moment, a pungent smell wafted out the cave, the wind spreading its stink. Tom flinched. He sucked in a ragged breath, lit the flashlight, and aimed it at the opening. "Presley?"

No response.

"You in there, buddy?"

Still nothing.

Whatever had happened in there, one part of Tom needed to get in, while another part of him didn't. But if he ever wanted to find Presley again, this could be his only chance.

Tom took a step in, directed the light forward, and the world on the outside welcomed a storm.

CHAPTER

21

THE FLASHLIGHT'S BEAM DIDN'T reach far into the cave, and the batteries still acted like they would die at any moment. But it was all Tom had. He had to hurry before the darkness gobbled him alive in there.

"Presley? It's me, buddy," he said in an uncertain voice. "You in here?"

No response.

Tom swallowed hard and directed the light onto the cold stone walls around. They were dented and covered in long white marks mixed with what looked like blood and dirt. What had happened?

He tiptoed farther into the cave, like an uninvited sibling.

Cobwebs hung around him like thin ropes, and the white, bloody marks on the walls stretched several feet long and in undulating patterns.

The inside of the cave spread wider than the entrance. The suffocating, rotten smell rotated in the dusty air as if it seeped from the walls. It stank like a mixture of hot iron, electricity, and salt water.

Outside, the wind whined and caused the trees to rattle in rhythm. Birds flew past the cave opening, cackling, and disappeared into the storm.

Tom shivered, and his pulse slammed in his throat like a ticking bomb.

A small, clicking pitter-patter against the cold ground sounded from somewhere in the cave.

Tom stopped.

It came from in front of him, *deeper* inside the cave, from somewhere in the darkness.

"Presley?"

But before he could even blink, a big, wet, brown rat came out from the darkness and ran past him with a squeaky scream. Tom shuddered and wailed out a sob from deep in his throat. If he had to decide which animals were the worst, it would be those damn rats. They were the animals of the condemned and had no use whatsoever. They did nothing more than bring destruction. He wasn't afraid of them, just disgusted by them. Once, he and Margaret had almost lost the place to the destruction of rats. The cursed creatures had gotten into the basement through a hole as big as a quarter, and gnawed through both the power line and insulation, which had cost thousands of dollars to repair. It took Tom weeks to clean the entire house; a must-do since rats could bring nasty sickness with them. Who knew what kind of bacteria rats in a cave, in the middle of nowhere, could carry? Even the air could be polluted from those bastards.

What if they had hurt Presley?

Tom directed the light forward again, now eager to get further in, when something flashed deep in the darkness. "Presley?"

Still no answer.

Tom pointed the pitiful beam toward the flashing object. As he moved toward it, a shivering wind blew past him. An arm's length away from the object was enough for his mouth to fall and sweat to dampen his hair. A small, chirping sound slid from his throat. He couldn't help but stare until his eyes watered and tears fell to the cave floor. On the ground in front of him, a pair of dirty jeans legs stuck out from the muddy ground beside some stones. Next to the pants lay a yellow sun-faded shirt—the sleeves had been torn or bitten to shreds. It reminded him of the floor of a typical teenage room, but he was far from any civilization now. Far from safe, warm homes with security alarms and locks on the doors. He was alone in a large and isolated godforsaken place where neither clothes nor traces of other people should have been able to exist. But they did, right in front of him. What the hell was going on?

A shivering vein of ice ran through his body, tickling his skin.

Getting scared, trucker?

Tom took a step closer to the dirty clothes, and the weak light fell on them. Dark mud, or blood, covered big patches of the clothes.

He bent down and grabbed the shirt. A woman's shirt. Stains covered the shirt, in some places as splashes, in other places as blotches, like countries on a map. But the largest of the spots had a hole in the middle.

He dropped the shirt and shuddered, before he glanced behind him.

On the outside, the wind tore through the forest's canopy. One part of him wanted to stay in the cave, while the other one, the rational, logical part, wanted to escape. But he couldn't leave now. He needed to find out if Presley was in there. The dog could be hurt.

Tom directed the flashlight deeper in, and another object flashed like before, next by the clothes. He shuffled his boot-clad feet and squinted. A brief wave of cold ran through him with the speed of a waterfall.

He bent down and picked up the flashing object. What it was, made him fall to his knees with a silent scream, lodged in his throat.

In his hand, he held Presley's leash.

"No." His eyes watered even more. "Please, no!"

Tom wrapped the leash around his left hand and started to shake, before he glanced around with the flashlight. How could it be possible? If Presley's leash was in there, where was the dog? Thousands of thoughts struck him at once. He wanted to rush farther in, but something made him hesitate. The collar? Where was Presley's collar?

Tom threw the filthy clothes aside. The collar wasn't anywhere around. Could it still be around Presley's neck? If it was, could it mean—he was still out there somewhere—*alive*?

A critical hope sprang up within Tom. He had followed Presley's barks, but never heard them inside the cave.

Tom turned around.

Birds screamed on the outside as if warning of the terror to come. Another light breeze whistled from somewhere inside the cave, echoing its way to him. It swept past him and continued out the entrance.

It's over, Tom.

Tom directed the now shaking light back into the cave. *"No."*

Another wet brown rat took off by his feet. This time, Tom shrugged off the sight, trying to control the tension in his body. He grimaced and kicked the rat right into the cave wall. The rat ejected a squeek, got up on its feet, and disappeared. How many rats could be in there? Could Presley—be in there—*with them*? Or could the dog be on the outside? Tom hesitated where to go.

He's dead, trucker! The rats are chewing on him right now!

"No!" Tom took another step forward and brushed by some unknown objects on the ground. He aimed the light down, unsure of what else could be there. Right behind the clothes there was something sharp and grayish. The object stood up from the ground, like a crooked flagpole. He frowned as a heat of fear crept up his neck. He kicked away the wet soil around it with his boot. There, in the acidic earth, lay an upper jaw with a human-like form. The sight of it obliterated his rationality and struck a panic inside him, like a screaming, overheated teapot on the stove.

A tingling sensation sizzled over his entire body. Whatever had happened inside that cave, somebody had paid for it with their life.

Tom pointed the beam at the jaw bone. The sight of it made the tingling sensation grow into a fuzzy weakness that permeated his muscles. The ground around him didn't contain only one bone. It was littered with them under the surface dirt, as if he had walked into a catacomb. Now his heart banged in his chest, and it was like he became smaller than ever. All around him, the light lit up broken skulls with vertebrae, teeth, leg and arm bones, even bone splitters, all covered under a fine layer of dust, as if they had been laying there for ages. But some, even if only a few, looked fresh, with dark, dried blood on them. The cave held a sinister darkness, and it continued stretching far into the mountain.

You're scared, trucker!

Tom's throat and mouth went dry as his stomach sank. Even if he wanted to turn around now and run away, he couldn't. As long as there was a possibility that Presley could be in there, he *had* to continue, no matter what.

His trembling legs took him farther into the cave, as goose bumps popped all over his body. The stench of decay grew.

"Presley?" His whispering tone disappeared within the cold, grey walls. "Please tell me you're here, boy."

Silence.

Even the birds on the outside silenced, while the wind disappeared in a short and toneless swirl, but replaced with a distant, slow scraping.

The sound moved closer.

Tom stopped and turned around. "Presley? Is that you?"

The scraping sound came closer.

"Presley?"

The sound became a dry and heavy shambling. Whatever it was, it came against the cave opening.

Tom walked backward with hesitating movements, but a misjudged step made his right leg give out, and he fell backward. He hit the cold ground, and the flashlight bounced out of his hand, shattering against the cave floor. He was plunged into complete darkness.

Good-bye, Tom.

"No!" he whispered, eyes wide open. He searched with the fingertips for whatever lay on the ground around him. A raw wind enveloped his numbed body. He shivered, as if frost formed in his already aching lungs, unable to identify the objects his fingers grazed.

Now, it's your turn, trucker!

The shambling sound grew stronger, together with a stifling noise.

Tom shook. Panic rushed through his body, but he still managed to get up on his knees. His pulse thundered in his ears, and sweat seeped through his already wet clothes. He slammed his moist palms on the rocky ground. Along with the stones, sand, soil, bones, and whatever else jabbed into his fingers.

He *needed* the flashlight.

The back of his hand smacked into something hard. The flashlight. He grabbed it, but the cursed lid had come loose. The batteries were no longer there. In the eternal black, it would be impossible to find them. He bit himself on the inside of the cheek and left the flashlight on the ground.

In the same moment, a silhouette shrank the light from the cave opening, and the sight drove a sharp nail of pain right through Tom's heart. His blood turned to ice, and every cell in his body imploded.

He laid still on the cave's cold ground and couldn't breathe. He clenched his jaw and squeezed the remaining air from his lungs. There was only one way out of there, and that was no longer the entrance.

Tom Richards crawled through the oppressive blackness on his knees, deeper into the cave, while bits of bone and stone pushed into his flesh.

Something had come to take him.

CHAPTER

22

THE WORLD AS TOM Richards once knew didn't longer contain the same rules. He was now stuck in nature, a place where no rules existed.

He crawled in panic, deeper into the oppressive blackness of the cave. He searched for any signs that could help him. Nothing. Thumping shocks went through his ears as sweat ran in his eyes. His mouth was so dry, he couldn't swallow. But he continued to crawl on his knees, hoping for survival. Hoping to get away from whatever was behind him.

The darkness suffocated him. His head pulsated, and a hissing noise escalated around him. He put his hands against his ears, pressed his eyes shut, and twisted his face into a grimace. But the hissing struck him like an invisible pain.

Scared, trucker? You should be! You fucking coward!

Behind him, a sickening grunt, followed by a crunching sound, echoed. Tom's chest rose and fell, increasing in speed, as his throat closed around his breath. He had to find an exit. But where?

You can't hide, trucker!

Tom clenched his jaws, and placed his palms against the cold, angular cave walls. He crawled deeper down the cave, while stones and bone fragments continued to penetrate his kneecaps. He pressed his lips together to avoid making audible groans. Where would the walls take him? It had to be an exit somewhere. There had to be because of the wind current, but the thought of traveling further in sickened his insides. What if the cave led him farther down into the mountain where no exit could be found at all? Lured deeper into the earth, he would be stuck forever—or until something found him. But he had no other choice. He had to get away from there. But without any light, he was in the hands of the cave.

That's when an idea occurred to him. As he continued following the wall, panting in panic, he pressed his hand inside his chest pocket, and searched for the cigarette package. The Zippo lighter could be his only key to a light source.

He pulled the lighter from the pack with stiff fingers and spun the spark wheel with his thumb. Nothing happened. He tried again. Still nothing.

You don't stand a chance, trucker!

Tom shook the lighter, blew on it, and pulled back the spark wheel once more. A vague blue flame morphed into a long red one. It ignited an inner hope in all the darkness. The lighter gave off just enough illumination for him to follow along the cave wall. He tracked the bloody white scratch marks deeper into the cave, unsure where they went.

A bright, razor-sharp sound appeared from the outside, shaped by the storm. A second later, a dark, ragged howl came in batches through the cave, like a ritualistic chant, first low, then with an increasing volume. With the growl, the intrusive smell of decay came back, as if it rose from the cave floor.

Tom's pulse rose with it.

He continued forward.

A light hissing sound of running water whispered through the wall. Tom moved a few inches farther. He closed in with his ear close to the rock wall. If there was water, it had to be an exit close by.

You won't find any exit!

Tom rocked back on his boots and stood. The sound of running water came closer the farther into the cave he went. There was no room for error. This could be his only chance out of there. One mistake and he would be a dead man.

Tom continued deeper, and one of his boots splashed into cold, gushing water.

He bent, moving the lighter closer to the running water. The liquid gushed farther down into the cave, deeper into the *unknown*. But the trail of the river turned left a few feet in. It would be risky to cross it. He could stumble on a wet stone revealing his location. But it was also risky going back … *no*…that was not an option. He *had* to tackle the water.

Barbaric grunts and thumps bounced off the cave walls.

The sounds came closer.

Whatever was in there with him, Tom clenched his jaws and forced himself through the cold, raging water. In one hand, he held the burning lighter, in the other one, he held the dangling leash from Presley. For each step he took, the metal clip on the leash struck the stone walls with a low clink.

He continued his sideways walk through the water with small steps. He breathed in shallow snatches and tried to focus. Couldn't afford to lose control. Not in *here*.

More howls.

Something at the corner of his eye caught his attention; deeper in the cave came a weak light from what could be a horizontal opening in the wall. Could it be an exit? A chance of hope lit inside him.

Tom hurried in the direction of the light. He tried to keep focus, but the cold water seeped into his skin, making him shiver.

The smell grew stronger. If it wasn't the water causing the wretched stink, it must be another dead carcass.

A heavy slam sounded from behind, together with a suffocating buzzing. In the same moment, a buzzing swarm of hungry flies surrounded him. Tom jerked his head back. The flies were the size of thumb nails and, no doubt, attracted to the horrible stench of rotting flesh and blood. The insects didn't leave him alone for a second; they attached themselves to him and followed him through the darkness. They tried to get into his mouth, ears, and nostrils. He spat, growled, and flailed his arms to remove them, all while trying to keep quiet. One of his boots kicked into something hard. Whatever it was, it flew against the wall with a hollow knock. It could have been a stone. Or a skull. Whatever he had kicked, it made an echo throughout the cave.

Tom froze, certain he'd been heard.

Well done, trucker! You're screwed!

At first, nothing but the sound of the running water and the buzzing swarm of flies appeared around him. But then an intersecting desperate growl sounded from across the cave, together with the crackling and slamming sound of increasing footsteps. Whatever it was, it wasn't human. And it wasn't from an animal either.

And it came closer.

CHAPTER

23

TOM HAD TO REACH the light source before it was too late.

He held the lighter in front of him, and his lungs squeezed the already tight air out. He moved as fast as he could toward the possible exit.

The sound of rapid, fleshy steps mixed with a low growling came closer.

Not fast enough, Tommie!

The water slowed Tom down, but he struggled against it. This couldn't be the end. He couldn't die there. Not in a cave filled with other bodies. Not far away from any civilisation. And not far away from both Margaret and Presley. *No*, he was supposed to die old, in their bed at home. That was his plan. That had always been his plan. But everything was about to fail.

Not here.

Not now.

Tom squinted when the cold water ran past the bottom of his legs. He swung his arms, slapped at his neck, and tried to scare away the swarm of hungry flies.

They refused to leave.

He had to get it together.

It's over!

Tom shut out the voice, bent down to the water, and angled the flame over the silvery surface. Stones the size of an adult hand shone through the bottom. One step wrong and he could be in big trouble. A jagged stone could cut his knees open and blood would streak into the water. Whatever was behind him would, in all likelihood, smell the blood or hear his pathetic groaning. But everything was a risk in the darkness.

Tom's pulse bounced faster.

He wasn't far away from the possible exit now. The fresh air filled his lungs.

And the footsteps came closer.

Tom couldn't turn around and exploit his fear. He had to pretend nothing was happening. Had to disconnect from the footsteps behind him. Had to...

You're going to die, trucker!

The water pressed itself against the walls with a low streaming, and the cursed flies refused to move along. They feasted on Tom as if he'd been the only living flesh they'd tasted in ages. He had to endure their blood-sucking presence.

Stay where you are, coward!

Tom banged into a sharp rock formation that jutted out from the wall, like the corner of a table, and winced. More damage to his battered body.

The exit was in front of him now. But a rough, tight passageway stood between him and freedom. The gap between the walls couldn't be bigger than a standard twelve inch ruler.

You won't fit, trucker!

Tom brought the lighter in front of him. The sight of the narrow tunnel made every thought he had left in his mind to explode. But it was his only chance away from there.

Behind him, the threatening steps came even closer.

Tom couldn't wait any longer.

An overwhelming wave of panic forced its way through him. He shoved the lighter back into his chest pocket and braced his boot against the wall.

There were no other options.

CHAPTER

24

TOM GRIPPED THE EDGE of the passage with his right hand. In the left hand he still held the leash, but it didn't stop him from using his fingers. He placed his left hand above his right and managed to pull up onto a wet stone while the water ran by. He grabbed an outcropping on the inside of the cave hole and pulled both arms in, and then his head. His muscles burned, and he clamped his teeth together.

Through the narrow opening, a dull shimmer covered the forest. The sun lay deep in shade. But the smell of fresh air circulated through the cave hole.

The clumsy sound of feet became more distinct, and distinctive moans echoed through the darkness.

The flies filled Tom's head with their constant humming. He pulled his entire chest into the opening, scraping his ribs against the edge. The tightness made him gasp for breath.

You're a stupid man, Tommie!

The narrow passage forced him to lay flat on his stomach with his head pointed forward. He couldn't do anything more than pull himself along with his arms. Each breath pushed his back against the rock above. His legs still dangled in the darkness.

A stupid man who can't even save his own dog!

A sucking sound echoed through the cave accompanied by the sound of bones being crushed in a fierce, angry wave.

The familiar sound rushed through Tom's soul. His heart pounded against the cave's tight cave walls.

He had to maintain control.

One, two, three.

Breath.

It's over!

Tom extended his right arm through the flat passage. Dust rushed up in front of the hole. Outside, the wind made the trees shake with a violent snatch. The air current sucked some of the flies out into the storm. Some still crawled inside his clothes and tried to see what was under his eyelids.

Tom gripped a sharp-edged stone in the passage and pulled himself forward. He leaned on his upper body and kicked his legs to gain extra power. He came a little bit closer to freedom—but not enough. He took a short, desperate breath as sweat stuck against his body. The whole mountain's weight lay on top of him by now. If the mountain shifted even just a slight bit, it would slowly squeeze him to death. His ribs would break apart and one side of his face would be imprinted against the passage's cold and dusty underside. He would only be capable of staring straight ahead as the darkness of death filled the exit and panic took over. Eventually, he would hyperventilate and his lungs would collapse.

He couldn't allow it to happen. He *had* to get out of there now.

Tom stretched his left arm and crammed his fingertips into a slit in the wall. He mustered his power, gritted his teeth, and hauled himself forward. His lower body scraped against the jagged mountain's interior, and his sweater pulled upwards as his flesh yielded into scratched and bloody skin. His hips hitched over the edge and into the tunnel with a snap. The waist of his jeans tore. The cold draft from outside fanned in through the hole. His muscles strained. His legs still dangled in darkness. He grabbed for more sharpened stone edges and continued to pull forward. The passage narrowed, and he couldn't longer turn his head in any direction. His cheek scrubbed against the surface. A stone edge pressed itself between his shoulder blades.

A little *more*.

His knees went over the edge, then his boots, one by one.

Behind him came the sound of splashing water.

It was close now.

Something scratched by Tom's boots, and his heart stopped for a second as dust went right up his nostrils. The air from the outside tousled his sweaty hair. With all his thoughts on Margaret and Presley, he stretched out his arms in desperation, out toward freedom. He pressed against the sides of the cave with trembling fingers. His body shook and burned with fatigue. The stone above tore a hole in the back of his shirt and punctured his skin like a bed of nails. He could no longer breathe. But nothing would stop him now. His right ear scraped against the surface with a scrunch as pain radiated through his left leg. His face flared with heat. It became tighter inside the passage the closer he came to the exit. He was filled with an intense desire for freedom. The flies that had stuck to his back continued to crawl on him.

You're never getting out alive from here!

Tom's elbows sought their way to the passage's exit. His knees bumped over the flesh-flaying surface. He strained his arms toward the exit, boot scraping along the tunnel walls. Finally, his hair reached freedom and fluttered in the breeze.

Just … a *little* bit … more.

Tom's head cleared the hole, and he gasped for breath, as if he had been locked in the mountain for years. The stone, which had torn apart his sweater, now sliced into the back of his thigh like the edge of a sharp axe. It cut right through his pants, down toward the knee joint. But he didn't stop. He continued to pull, and his shoulders popped out into freedom, one by one. Grabbing at the ground outside, he once again pulled with everything he had left in him. His muscles seared with the constant lactic acid, and his chest popped out of the exit. The rest of the body was wedged in the rock still, and he now hung, half in half out of the tunnel.

Something inside scratched at his boot again.

From behind Tom, deep in the passage, a dark, wheezing voice whispered, "I see *you*."

Panic rushed through Tom as if he had fallen against an electric fence. He kicked his legs backward and shoved himself forward while his pulse hammered from all places. The stone, which had penetrated his leg, now cut deeper into him. At that moment, something cracked behind him. Tom closed his eyes, clenched his teeth, and made one final pull.

The stone piece, which had prevented him from moving forward, broke loose, and he fell into the outside air. It all happened so fast, his perception didn't follow when he landed and smashed his shoulder into a tree stump with a crack. The force made him roll into the shadows. The grass surrounded him, as he filled his lungs with the sweet aroma of the pine forest. A woodpecker welcomed him back to the atmosphere of peace. It tapped and rattled its beak among the beauties of nature, and the wind pulled at his ragged clothes. Even though he lay undercover of a few branches, the rain still wet his skin. For Tom Richards, the world had once again become a pleasant field of treasures, even if another storm was brewing. And even though the world still possessed secrets, at least he wasn't stuck in the cave anymore.

But then he lifted his shaking head and stared into the darkness of the cave hole. A broad and unnatural smile shone back at him from the black, like the shape of a sharp, rusty scythe. A few cracked, uneven teeth protruded from the creatures rotting gums, which were covered in an almost silvery membrane, streaked with blood and mucus. The creature's jaw creaked open, and it whispered, "I want—the *dog*." The voice had a croaking, throaty sound as if it had been squeezed out from a sealed, rotten coffin, deep down underground, where troubled spirits still grew to the sounds of crawling insects.

Tom struggled for his breath, as he crawled backward on his elbows.

"The *dog!*" the creature groaned, and its broad smile lost its arch-like shape. "Give it… to *me*."

Tom crawled backward until he slammed into a conifer, and even though the impact made him gasp for his breath, he continued to stare into the shaded cave opening.

The creature shrieked in delight, and a scrawny arm with crooked, bony fingers stretched its way out from the hole, grasping after him.

Tom pulled himself up with the tree, turned around, and ran into the forest.

He didn't look back, not even once.

CHAPTER

25

THERE HAD BEEN MOMENTS in Tom Richards life that had flown by as if the clock was spinning faster than time allowed. But these last couple of months, his own clock, the one inside him, slowed to a crawl. As he now ran along the shady forest, and the rain clouds swept south, that slow-motion feeling came back, and it was like he floated in the air. A chilled breeze pulled through him, but the adrenaline flowing through his veins forced him to continue. The wind carried the spicy but pleasant smell of pollinated flowers. But whichever way he turned, it all had the same superficial look. For the first time since escaping the cave, he dared to take a real breath. But it hurt more than it provided relief.

With no idea where he was going, Tom turned his way north into the forest, where he forced himself through worn-out ferns and tangled plants. From there, he crawled under a fallen pine and into the untamed nature like a frightened animal. Twigs slapped him in the face and tore up his already damaged clothes. For a few seconds, a strong headwind froze his joints. He searched for somewhere to shelter; his pulse pounded like a drumbeat inside him. He had *nowhere* to shelter—to *hide*. Danger lurked everywhere.

Sinkholes traversed the grounds, and angular tree breaks waited for him to fail. He could be killed faster than he would be capable of reacting.

You can't escape from here!

Tom held his palms against his ears, and begged the voice to stop, while he continued farther into the dense forest of the fossilized environment. The trees were swaying as if they were readying to move against him. Bushes with thorns ensnared his feet. Branches hung, prepared to capture him alive. Roots reached across the ground, ready to trip him. He had to zig-zag until his stomach cramped and forced him to his knees.

He placed his sweaty palms among the untroubled plants, and another puke shot through him without warning. Another yellow slime of bile hung loose from his bottom lip. He spat out the hanging yellow phlegm, and his head spun like a carousel again. The adrenaline was on the edge of ending, and it made his sight blurry. He *had* to find protection, to cover himself. But the part of the forest he now stood in was too sparse to hide him. He had to move on to a more sheltered spot, somewhere far from the cave, perhaps even *farther* from Presley. But he needed to get away from whatever lived inside that cave.

There's no place for you to hide!

Tom got up on his trembling legs as a red hot pain shot like a hammer blow down his spine. His shoulders burned and his body stiffened while his head continued to swim in giddy waves. The forest concealed the darkness and allowed only glimpses of its true nature. Inviting green conifers spread coarse branches and shadowed sharp rocks.

He stopped, bent down, and crouched forward against a long, fallen tree trunk. It had turned gray during the torments of the season. The visible root system looked like hundreds of snakes searching for a tunnel to the underground world.

He secured himself behind the windproof, multi-armed wonder and tried to control his breathing. All thoughts and sensations blurred into one. His slimy throat made it hard to catch any breath. His eyes were filled with tears. He still had Presley's leash wrapped around his left hand, and he couldn't stop thinking about how it had gotten *inside* the cave, of all places. Tom squeezed it in his hand and made his already white fingertips, which were wrinkled like an old person's face, throb even more. Why did the evil creature want Presley? But if it wanted Presley, it meant the dog could still be alive out there somewhere. But the question was—*where*? And how would Tom find him?

One of the cursed flies crawled out from under Tom's shirt. When it reached his neck, he smacked it and muted its whirring. Tom stretched out his palm in front of his face. The black, two-winged creature lay there with convulsive legs in a smear of blood, its wings flattened, those convulsing legs now broken sticks pointed in different directions.

Tom squeezed his eyes shut as his lips rose upwards into a smile. He leaned his pounding head back toward the hard, snake-like branches and stared up at the swaying canopy. A laugh bursted out of him. If nature and everything it contained wanted to kill him, it would have to try harder.

Before gathering his thoughts, Tom rose to his feet with the help of the roots on the underside of the trunk. Guided by a subconscious force, he wandered back out into the unknown forest. The force took him where he couldn't go himself. He half-jumped over the shaded woodland as the dark clouds passed over the swaying silhouettes of the tree tops. The wind pushed him forward together with the rain.

It wouldn't be long until the darkness once again fell in Alaska. And the days would only become shorter and colder.

Tom had to find Presley before the creature did. But to what price?

CHAPTER

26

THE NATURE IN ALASKA didn't only consist of the forest itself anymore. It brought many deadly traps, traps that through years of natural progression and climate, made no human able to conquer it. And it also brought evil forces, forgotten, or distressed by the normal world — forces, that for a long time ago, should have been conquered.

So far, Tom had managed to survive in the nature and the evil creature inside the cave. But what more hid out there?

Tom now followed along a length of swaying trees against a slope southeast of the cave. His best chance to find Presley out there was still with the view from a mountain, but all thoughts of going to any other mountain caused his body to shake with fear. All he needed now was to get far away from the cave that could have become his death. But sooner or later, he had to swallow his fear and get out of any kind of convenience struggling against him. But wherever he now went, Presley could be anywhere, dead or alive. Something he didn't want to think about.

Tom stopped by a slope. Hundreds of years before him, the ground had been home to animals now extinct, some preserved beneath the front edges of the slope. The slope continued downward twisting with grass and fallen tree branches.

He glanced out over the mysterious tree-filled landscape, and thought about Margaret. If the place wasn't full of evil, it would be a place Margaret would've loved to see; the light illuminated the passing, obscure clouds, as the wind blew waves of light-headed trees with a few raindrops threatening to increase in quantity. Groups of birds flew in various directions. Beautiful enough to be painted on a canvas. All alive, but still filled with the darkness of death.

The thought of Margaret could sit there for a whole day to paint, made Tom laugh a brief one. Margaret's interest in painting had come when she discovered her father's rectangular wood box, with artist accessories, in the attic, one year after they took over the farm. To Margaret's delightful surprise, the box had been filled with everything from watercolor brushes in hard hair and squirrel hair, to dozens of unused color tubes, palette knives, granulating agents, a bottle of ox gall, and oils she even couldn't pronounce the names of. Throughout the years, art had relieved her depression over being unable to get pregnant and the fresh grief for the loss of her father. Mr. Wilson had been a pleasant man and a hard-working watchmaker, who, most of the time, kept to himself. Margaret didn't have too many stories about him. Her parents had divorced before she turned five. Her mother had escorted her and everything they possessed to west Alaska. The fact that the father, almost fifteen years later, had left the farm to her had come as a surprise. At first, everything was good on the farm, just like Mr. Wilson had wanted it to be. Tom and Margaret's marriage was good, the sex was fantastic, the garden was fresh and green, yes, even the neighbors, the Brown's, had been good friends, even though they acted weird. But like a slow leak in a boat, water overcame them and caused them to sink; the arguments in their relationship escalated, the problems got bigger, the constant control of each other grew worse, and everything led to more troubles. They tried marriage counseling, but Margaret was never present. One day Margaret wanted to divorce and Tom agreed. Everything had gone too far. Their attempts at having children had slowly torn apart their marriage like chewing gum pulled at each end. But like everything else in the Richards family, when accidents happened, it had been postponed. The marriage paper had been put in a box in the basement, and shortly thereafter, the rats had invaded the basement. In addition to destroying the electricity and all those holes in the walls, the rats also chewed up the marriage paper and other documents. Margaret had perceived it as a sign from above, how the rats were somehow there to bring them together again, whether they wanted it or not. And it somehow forced them to clear up the situation together. Tom worked while Margaret took care of the home. After the repair, they agreed they couldn't live without each other again. But like one day to the other, the economy collapsed, and Tom had to take on other jobs in addition to his usual work hours, which left no time for leisure. He had to stop working on the pickup in his spare time and, instead, he had to earn more money by trucking. Even Margaret had to stop painting. All talk about children remained far beyond their reach. In spite of this, more and more weaknesses emerged in their relationship: the lack of sleep, the disappearing of the social life, people started talking behind their backs. Tom lost faith in everyone, except for Presley. Who knew what would have happened if they hadn't decided to get the dog? Tom and Margaret found their way back to each other. They accepted the fact they would never have their own children. With Presley, things got better. Tom and Margaret even started to have sex again. They regained what they had lost somewhere along the road, and they both realized the world consisted of both good and bad parts. Even the beer came to taste better for a period of time. But then it happened again, when the economy sank again. The bills could be seen as the completion of an evil circle. It seemed as if Wilson was punishing them from the grave, and anxiety knocked on Tom like the lid to a coffin. His focus disappeared, and the loneliness grew stronger than before. Sleep disturbances came more often. The mood swings. Problems with relationships outside his private life. The whole practical world disintegrated. But they had to work out the problems themselves. They didn't need any economical help, especially not from Margaret's mother. Tom dug himself deeper into the earth, to a place he didn't believe existed inside mortal minds. If everything had its explanation and cause, it was based on emotional cases, and only a degenerate evil could follow. But then the damn offer had come. The cursed offer which could bring him and Margaret out of debt, at least for a period of time. It would just be a simple trip down the Dalton highway and back. No big deal. An express delivery. Two days. Easy as a pie. When Tom accepted it, it was like a weight released from his shoulders and another turn for the better life had arrived. But the world had other plans for him.

As Tom now stood there on the edge of the slope, with the wind fluttered through his hair, he was nothing but a lost man. He needed to get back home. It was he and Margaret against the world, and Presley was their little sidekick, like his own Robin, Luigi, or even Dr. Watson. But as one, they would tackle whatever came their way.

Within a few hours, the day would turn into night, light dimming into darkness. He had to find the dog before it was too late. But without the flashlight, and still without a weapon by his side, the night would make it hard to find Presley and even harder to defend himself from whatever belonged to the forest. The dangers out there grew stronger, and Tom didn't even know half of them. But nothing would stop him now. If he had gone this far, he could go much farther. It was a matter of mental force, an unbroken skill that flourished through empirical knowledge. But did he have what it takes?

Down by the slope, further into the forest, groups of animals passed with the autumn turning into winter.

Tom pulled the cigarette pack from his chest pocket and opened it up.

Three cigarettes left. One was nearly crushed.

He took out the broken cigarette and lit it. The smoke expanded his lungs and almost made him drunk.

Once again, he glanced through the forest. That's when George Goldman, once again, slipped through his memory. How much did the old man really know about the place?

Tom inhaled, and the smoke caused his body to relax for a moment. He should have listened to George, but it was all too late now.

Growing up as the only child with his mother and father on a farm, in a town west of Fairbanks, had made Tom familiar with the forest and what it contained. As a child, his family lived near the Alaska Railroad, the state-owned railroad that stretched from southern Alaska in Seward beyond the Fairbanks final destination in the north. From the farm they could follow a part of the track before it disappeared behind a forest grove a few yards from there, a place Tom never was allowed to visit alone. Too dangerous for a kid. Tom's father, Bernie Howard, had bought the farm with thirty acres a few years before Alaska became an official state in 1959. Bernie had bought the farm for a reduced price but had been forced to rebuild most of the house after the Great Alaska Earthquake of 64, which affected most of the Anchorage area with catastrophic consequences and left other parts of Alaska unaffected.

Tom inhaled the cigarette and glanced out down the slope again, following the wind through the forest, unsure what to believe. But it was in that moment it came to him, like a fish that nibbled on the bait, but couldn't do anything about it because the hook was already digging into the jaw, that something must have happened with the Dalton Highway-area during the violent earthquake of 64. It must have been then, when the earth cracked open, the creature in the cave crawled up from hell. And if it came from hell, it could only mean one thing.

It had to be the Devil.

Tom now shook even more. But could it be possible? His parents had told him what it meant to be a good Christian, even though they never followed the advice they gave him. Each man did what God led him to do, as long as he took care of his family. Bernie, a man of faith, taught Tom about the importance of God and the importance to provide for his family. He had warned Tom about how evil could be lurking in every corner in the world, and it would be a mistake not to believe in the bad powers in life if you believed in the good ones. Had those lessons led to this moment? But everything that happened to him must have meant something.

Tom tried to think. Could it all be planned? Had he been sent out there to do God's work? Was he the chosen one?

Now, as Presley hopefully ran around somewhere out there, lost and freezing in such a mass expanse, Tom couldn't believe what he had been through. He brought Presley out there, and he would take him home again. But for an unknown reason, the Devil wanted the dog as much as he did. Was the dog nothing but bait?

Tom needed to produce a plan, which at least would be better than nothing at all for the moment.

He fingered the outside of his shirt, where the package of cigarettes lay, and a smile worked its way across his lips. How well would the Devil stand against fire, after all? What if the hell didn't contain any fire at all, as everybody thought, but instead was a cold, miserable, damp crust?

A laugh bubbled up through Tom's throat. If he did what he was sent here to do, they might leave him alone.

PART THREE

CHAPTER

27

IN A MATTER OF hours, another cold, dark September night would sweep over Alaska's landscapes, and Tom Richards would be forced to get rid of the Devil and find Presley before then.

Tom staggered down the sloping terrain, through a wild forest with low-hanging tree branches, which made shadows dance along the unharvested undergrowth. Rain clouds penetrated the churning sky, as a breeze with the sweet smell of citrus passed by. The trees at the edge of the horizon spiked like a dragon's talons.

But something on the other side of the overgrown branches and foliage shimmered like thousands of silver spoons.

He peeked through the overgrowth. A wind swept past him and made him squint.

Even though he needed to find Presley, he still had an inner temptation to get there; the thought of water made his dry throat ache.

He coughed, hesitating for a second. Drinking water from a lake could be dangerous. The water could be filled with all sorts of bacteria and toxic substances, but his dry throat ached. What other choices existed? Dying of thirst could take days.

Long days.

Tom glanced down to the lake again. It glittered at him, almost welcoming him.

He had to drink. But he had to hurry. When darkness fell, the Devil would be the one who ruled out here, and Tom was on his playground. In addition to the dropping temperature, the intrusive night shadows would also trick the predator's hungry mouths into action. In the mysterious power of nature, he had to choose between being the hunted or become the hunter. Without a weapon, he would be an easy victim for anything out there. The only thing he could use was his Zippo lighter. With the lighter, he could make a torch and protect himself with the fire as long as the rain didn't destroy it. Everything would fear him with the fire by his side. But did that include the Devil?

The area Tom staggered through shifted color, and when he reached a tree, which lay in pieces on the ground, a buzzing sound filled his ears. First it rotated around his head with a distant vibration then grew stronger, drilling deeper into his skull. It was the hiss of whispers, and the force of their message made him lean against the split-open tree bark of a nearby spruce, a place where insects had barricaded themselves from the Alaskan chill.

Can you handle this?

Don't screw this up.

Your dog is dead! Don't you get that?!

Tom pressed his sweaty palms against his numb ears. "Leave me!" He cowered, worried the voices would eat him from the inside out. He groaned and closed his eyes. A migraine exploded in his head. The whispers flashed through the corners of his mind like clips from an old talkie.

You're a dead man!

A pulsating flow of dread coursed through his spine, all the way up to his skull, where the buzzing made him twitch and sink to the ground. The sharp blades of grass and undergrowth sliced at his face, the fresh cuts stinging with exposure.

In an instant, the buzzing whispers vanished on the wisps of the wind.

Tom took a deep breath. It jarred his chest, and his forehead dampened when the humid air engulfed him. An icy breeze escalated through the forest, and the autumn leaves and sticky, sharpened pine needles fell down on him.

No.

He had to continue.

In the remote forest around Dalton highway, where the sun sometimes created a green and unspoiled cover of the landscape, and other times nothing but darkness, Tom hurried down the last part of the forest, despite the grass that tugged at his legs. His muscles burned, making tears of sweat attack his skin.

He half-jumped through the grass when he lost his balance, stumbled, and got cut on his cheek by something in the grass. The skin on his cheek hung open in a flap about the size of a coin, and warm blood trickled down onto both his face and clothes. The grass folded around his body and pricked his skin. He cursed, and then pulled himself up. He pushed himself through the last few feet.

His eyes flickered. He had to have water—now—before he died of thirst.

Tom ran, with heavy legs, tossing the leash on the ground as he went. He dropped to his knees by the water's edge, the same position he had formed as a kid when his parents had told him to pray before bedtime. He cupped his dirty hands, like the bucket of an excavator, and shoveled the ice-cold water into his dry mouth. As the water reached his throat, he started to cough. The liquid made his lungs twist and his stomach cramp. The water mixed with his blood seeped through the hole in his cheek, and the wound pounded. More of the water splashed back into the lake or onto his already wet clothes. He didn't care.

Tom let out a low groan while he repeated the movement over and over again until he no longer could lift his arms. How much water did he dare to drink before he would puke it up? He didn't care if it was bacteria ridden longer. He satiated his unpleasant thirst. But a sudden movement on the water's surface made him stiffen. A blurred image emerged from the surface of the turbid water. Tom frowned, but the face in front of him didn't. The face in front of him, instead, had a distorted and unknowable structure to it. It was the face of a scrawny, brown-haired boy with big blue eyes, and he stared back at him. The boy raised his eyebrows upwards while his mouth stood open like a birdhouse, as if something was about to happen. The boy's frightened face made Tom's own turn with terror.

It was himself.

"No," Tom whispered. His arms lost strength, and he fell into the water, where the underwater grass folded around him and gripped tight. His lungs filled, and every cell in his body vibrated in panic. He struggled to the surface and gasped for breath. In a clumsy movement, he crawled back on land and searched the surface wide-eyed, but all it showed was the reflection of the cloudy sky.

Tom got up on his knees, placed his fingers on his face, and searched it as if he were a blind person inspecting a newcomer. His stiff beard scratched his fingertips as he ran them across his jaws all the way to the bloody wound on his cheek. His nose was still the size of a grown man's, and he still had the same cracked lips as earlier. The wrinkles by his eyes were the same, too. The face he touched couldn't be mistaken for a child's. He wasn't a kid anymore. He couldn't stand to suffer through that period again.

A dark noise, like the humming from a far-off engine, bubbled out of him. It was his own laugh. The monotonic, guttural sound came with no control. Tom stuffed his dirty fingers in his mouth to quiet himself, but the laugh fell out with such intensity it made him fall forward into the sand-mixed soil in cramps. He rolled over to the side, put his arms over his stomach, and kicked like a defiant child. Nothing made sense anymore. The world didn't consist of the world any longer. The landscape around could be seen as a divine wealth with nature's almost perfect creations of peculiar plants and living things, but somewhere, deep within the core of the earth, also radiated a mysterious darkness that affected the earth's natural patterns. In the most beautiful light, a dull whispering also existed, which sought its way among the bright streaks of Tom's shrinking reality. Surprises lurked around every corner, mystique behind every horror.

Tom stopped laughing. He got to his feet and brushed off the heavy soil from his damp clothes. Water still dripped from his damaged cheek. He bent down and picked up the leash. The wound on his cheek pulsed with the movement. His wet hair lay in curls against his forehead. If he had ever needed his cap, now would be that time. But the cap was out there in the forest somewhere, abandoned, like Presley. The thought stabbed into him like a twisting knife in the heart.

He glanced at the glittering lake, and it rippled with calm waves. But the light the reflections gave, made him turn to the forest again. It wasn't until then he got a glimpse of something in the west end of the forest, deeper in.

Something woke inside Tom, like a glow that was dying out but once again drew oxygen and came back to life.

He walked against the trees, peered through the branches that hung in front of him, through berry-laden bushes, and along a broad wall of brush. What was in front of him, made his blood pulse through his veins and his eyes filled with tears.

There, under an overgrown shrub, lay Presley.

28

WITH A CRY IN his throat and on the verge of totally losing it, Tom sprang from the ground and staggered forward. He hurried against the bushes, and a band of steel released itself in his chest. Could his sight be telling him the truth, or could it be some kind of mirage, where a desperate hope had gripped his mind and overpowered his sensibilities?

He stopped, rubbed his palms against his teary eyes, and blinked. When he regained focus, Presley still lay there on the spongy ground, dappled by the shadows from the bushes. The dog stared at him, but didn't come. Instead, he had a certain hesitation in his gaze, as if Tom was a stranger. Didn't the dog recognize him?

Tom scrunched up his eyebrows.

Presley had changed; his golden and black fur, was now greasy with smeared spots of mud over his back and face. His ears were covered in a black sooty substance, and his face had a scruffy appearance. The dog's mouth hung wide open with threads of saliva hanging against the ground.

It's not your dog, Tommie! Can't you see that? Your dog is dead!

Tom stood in the swaying grass, and a wave of caution rinsed through him. He hesitated to go any farther in case Presley had turned into a menacing beast. Instead, Tom stretched out his hand as if he held a treat. "Presley," he whispered. "Come to me—buddy. It's *me*. We have to get away from here. *Now*."

Presley didn't move. In the dog's pitch-dark eyes appeared a reflection of the raging sky. But something else reflected in those eyes, too, something in the distance.

The dog started to growl and backed away from the bushes, away from Tom.

"Presley?" Tom blubbered with his eyebrows raised. "Stay, buddy. It's *me*. You don't need to be afraid." He went after him, tears filling his eyes. He dropped the leash. It caught in some bushes and dangled in the air. Tom snatched it up. The dog continued backward, and his growl grew darker and heavier, coming from deeper in his throat. He flattened his ears against his filthy head, scrunched up his nose, and pulled his lips into a snarl.

"Presley, you don't need—" Then it hit Tom. He turned and the sight down by the water made his limbs turn into ice.

The Devil's stiff form appeared where Tom had been kneeling and drinking water only moments before. The faded light shone on his pale and grayish face. But what was most distinctive was his clothing; he wore a dusty white shirt that appeared to be stained with dirt and other substances, a torn sweater, rags of a copper colored vest, and a pair of soiled and worn black costume pants that came up above his waist. But the same wicked smile Tom had seen in the cave, revealed it was the Devil.

A rattling noise tore Tom's attention back to Presley. The dog was running away.

Tom's heart pounded inside him like a boxer punching a speed bag.

No.

He couldn't let the dog escape again.

Tom staggered after Presley.

And the Devil followed.

CHAPTER

29

IN TOM'S MIND, HE had escaped from the Devil at the cave, but the Devil had followed him the entire time, concealed behind the swaying shadows and dense plants. He had stalked Tom until he had brought him to Presley.

In that moment, not much existed for Tom Richards anymore. Nothing more than the wind, which rippled through his clothes in silent waves, as the chill bit into his skin. All sounds melted into the seductive darkness, as if someone had thrown a blanket over the whole forest.

Tom stumbled after Presley. His boots and tired muscles made him clumsy. But he couldn't give up, no matter how much he wanted to. He ran after the dog until he tripped on a curved root, and crashed to the ground. He struggled to his feet again with the help of some thickets of weeds.

You won't make it, Tommie!

The Devil stalked him from behind emitting short, monotonic clucks that grew in volume.

Presley ran easy on his paws, and Tom dragged himself a few feet along the tree line. There was no chance at catching Presley. But if he didn't, he might never see the dog again. A scared animal could hide anywhere, if he succeeded without getting caught. But the forest was no place for a chase.

The only way to shake the Devil was to hide from him again. But Tom still needed to get to Presley before doing so.

As Tom followed the dog past cracked coniferous trees, and passed the strange formations nature offered as art, twigs snapped and bushes rattled closer and closer behind him.

He glanced around.

No, no.

Tom's pulse bounced in his throat, and he lost his rhythm for a second. He glimpsed the Devil, with his pale skin and an expression indicative of the limits of suffering. The Devil groped at him with his long, skeletal fingers.

They weren't more than a bus length away from each other, but the Devil came closer.

Tom continued after Presley with heavy legs.

The dog stopped and glanced at Tom with a heavy panting. His wet eyes reflected the dimming light from the spreading rain clouds above, and the whole forest silenced. It was as if the sound had been sucked out, as if the forest life had disappeared like a rocket into outer space.

This could be his only chance, the moment he had waited for.

Tom gripped the leash in his hand and directed the collar toward Presley's neck, ready to connect him. He came closer, and when their eyes met, the fear stilled. If it weren't for how Tom trampled down the unstable gravel, things might have been solved and come to an end, but instead he fell to the ground with a short, howling scream. He lost sight of Presley while the trees around him stretched to the sky. The wild grass tangled around him, as the crooked tree roots snaked over him and pulled him underground. He disappeared beneath the damp muck, swallowed whole.

Above the ground, Presley escaped the sinkhole with a bark, and seconds later, rapid footsteps came close.

Tom smacked between walls of soil while sharpened stones tore up his already battered flesh. He sank deeper into the cold dank, until he got stuck.

A shadow lowered over Tom, as if the night had come, and everything blackened.

CHAPTER

30

TOM STOOD QUIET BY the cave entrance, when a hoarse whisper called his name from inside.

He turned on the flashlight and went in. Rats fled, passing him, one by one. They squealed.

"Hurry, Tom!" the voice from the inside of the cave shouted. "The rain will make you cold! I've got some buns and hot chocolate waiting for us in here!"

Tom followed the female voice deeper in, but a group of flies attacked him and whispered into his ears, "He'll kill you, Tom. He'll kill you, Tom! HE'LL KILL YOU, TOM! AND HE'LL FEED US WITH YOUR WORTHLESS BODY!"

He slapped away the flies. They fell to the ground and made the piles of discarded bones shake with false life.

Tom walked beside the bloody claw marks on the wall, but this time, when he directed the flashlight against the rock, they weren't claw marks. Instead, a bloody text read: "HAVE YOU SEEN MY BROTHER, JACOB WILKINS?", "MISSING", "666" and "PLEASE HELP ME FIND MY DAUGHTER!"

The deeper into the cave as Tom went, the more the light from his flashlight started to give up. He hit it, and the light pulsated.

Then it went black.

In the same moment, something snapped inside the cave, like the sound of a twig breaking.

"It's so lonely over here," the woman said. "Please don't leave me alone here. I got cookies over here. Do you like cookies, Tom? I do. I like cookies. Why don't you come over here and taste some?"

The whispering sizzled like an electric shock through the air. It took him from nausea to prolonged, tired panting.

"Why aren't you coming, Tom? I want you to come here!"

It solidified his joints, and he couldn't move a single muscle.

It was in that moment something grabbed his right leg. It first came like a slight jerk, as if Tom had gotten stuck in something on the ground, like a twisted root, but the jerks grew stronger with each passing second. It didn't take long before the discomfort turned into a screeching pain that flashed around the narrow bone and up against his hip.

Tom pulled back his leg and tried to snatch, tear, do everything in his power to get free, but without results. His flashlight lit up again, and what was below him made him gasp. Someone crawled on the floor and pulled him downward. The skin on the person's fingers hung loose, like threads from a rag rug. It was like someone had put the fingers in a pencil sharpener.

Tom tried to scream, but what came out was a strangled whimper into empty darkness.

The hand yanked Tom down to the ground.

In pure reflex, he shot out his arms as protection, but he still hit his back on the ground with a jolt. The flashlight flew out of his hand, and for a brief moment, when the light shone just right, he recognized the bony, stubborn face. It was Miss Paterson. Her jaw swung loose, as if it had been torn free. Out of her mouth hung a bloated, purpled tongue that dangled like a dead fish. Her upper lip had been worn all the way up to her flattened nose and exposed the sight of a dark, hollow palate with rotten black gums and decaying teeth. Where her eyes once had been, now there was nothing more than excavated, vacant holes, filled with what looked like clumps of soot and rancid coffee beans, mixed up with solidified blood and a stinking, slimy yellow seepage. Across her forehead, her skin split in an angry gash that disappeared into her stringy, long hair.

"The Devil," she whispered in a dry, low-key groan. "Why didn't you warn me before, Tom? Why? Tell me why, your son of a bitch!"

Tom's neck strangled with an overwhelming and stifling fright. He slid backwards on his elbows, backwards toward the light from the entrance.

Miss Paterson curved her rotting hands and grabbed along Tom's quaking legs. "The Devil!" she crouched, as her tongue dangled like an immobile slug. "In the end, he'll take us all!"

Tom tried to kick off the dead woman's grip, but his legs had no strength left. It was like they were made from jelly. "Get away from me!"

Miss Paterson's fingertips dug deeper into his shins, as her dead face waggled in the dimly illuminated cave.

"Only you can stop him, Tom!" She shouted. "Only you can save us all!"

Tom squeezed his eyes shut, as Miss Paterson crawled up; the skin of her face flapped against Tom. "Save us all from evil!"

Tom tensed his muscles and managed to shove Miss Paterson's body back into the darkness, and for a short moment, the empty black swallowed them both. Whatever it was that had appeared in front of him, it couldn't have been Miss Paterson.

From the dark, a short, strangled cry echoed.

The walls shook as cold ground vibrated beneath Tom's feet. The roof trembled, on the verge of collapsing.

CHAPTER

31

TOM SNAPPED HIS EYES open and gasped when a landslide fell over him. Quiet had returned, but this time it brought the stale smell of dead roots. The stink of muscle cream and antiseptic pressed into his lungs. Was he in the dead ones' waiting room? Could it be his time now?

A strange sound snapped him back to reality. His vision flared in the light glaring through the hole above. But the Devil's silhouette also appeared up there, and his ears protruded at odd angles while his lips twitched outward in a wide grin. "Now ... the dog is all *mine,*" the Devil whispered. "I need to ... *have* it."

The Devil's voice seeped into Tom's veins, and all of his movement stiffened. The Devil's voice was a raspy, dry groan, and his teeth seemed too big for his mouth.

The Devil raised his arms towards the sky, spread his gnarled fingers, and gyrated his hips in a circle. He raised his knees up in the air, as if he danced for Tom. But the body movements were jerky and impaired, and the solitary squish from his feet stamping against the moist earth made Tom's insides twist.

Tom's cells rushed in panic when soil clumps fell down the hole, as if the Devil tried to bury him alive down there.

The earlier stench reappeared inside the cave, stronger now, hot contamination mixed with a chemical betrayal. The Devil moved faster, his feet stumbled on the ground, around and around in circles. He flung his arms in the air and kicked his legs. In addition to the subdued sounds of his feet thumping against the ground, words fell from the Devil's rotting mouth. The words didn't seem to be any language Tom could recognize, but they stung his ears with a nauseating pain.

Tom tried to move, but he was trapped. He lowered his head, and the dirt clods hit him in the back of the neck. His arms and legs shook as he searched the darkness for something to grab, something to help him *escape*. But the darkness covered everything, and the walls squeezed in on him.

"Please!" Tom tried to scream, but his throat burned like a parched flower in need of a drink before it collapsed, dropped its leaves, and shriveled into oblivion.

A sound echoed throughout the forest. The Devil froze, like an animal caught in the headlights. He turned from the hole to the forest, and puffed out his chest, ready for battle. The noise echoed again, like if someone had opened a rusted, iron door to another world. But it was Presley's bark.

Another bark broke the chilled silence, but it was lighter and shriller in tone.

Tom stared upward, expecting the Devil's shadowed form to be gone. It wasn't. Instead, the Devil thrust his thin, angular face toward him. His eyes were nothing more than bleached white balls with ruptured blood vessels; they rolled back into his head. His wrinkled, liver-colored lips formed an O. His pale skin had a waxy sheen like a cheap, plastic doll, and it was stretched tight over his lumpy face, which revealed his big, rotten, and sharp teeth. The Devil crackled, "I think— it's *here*."

Tom stared at the Devil, paralyzed. His eyes bulged, and his mouth ran dry, as he, for a second, lost all connection to his muscles. Piss ran down his leg. And with a swoosh, the Devil pulled himself back into the cold air, creaking out laughter, as a wide smile split his face. He jumped away from the hole.

Tom sank to the bottom of the hole, and his tears dripped down his face, mixing with the ever-invasive rain.

Somewhere in the forest, another bark snapped out.

And the Devil's feet hurried toward it.

CHAPTER

32

WITH THE DEVIL GONE, Tom could see outside. Gnawed plants and insects bordered the hole's edge. The sun still hid behind a group of grey cotton clouds, and the wind swept past with a silent force. The sky split open, and the drizzle increased to a thundering pour.

Tom tried to cover his face, but the water splattered him, blinding him, no matter which way he turned. He gasped from the shock of the cold drops.

Panic rushed his body.

He strained his arms upward, and his muscles burned like lit torches. Any movement made his limbs quake in misery. A stone pressed against his lower back while a branch or root of some kind dug into his left shoulder. For every breath he took, a razor sharp cut went right through him and jabbed deeper into his lungs, which swelled in his already mauled body. He was caught between two tapered walls, and the only way out was back where he fell. But he had to be quick. He didn't have much time left. He had to find Presley before the Devil did, but also before the walls collapsed and buried him alive.

See what you've done, trucker! It's all your fault!

Tom clenched his teeth and stared hard into the darkness. His head throbbed, and the rain made him narrow his eyes to slits. A few feet above him, Presley's leash dangled, caught on some twisted roots. If he could grab it, he might be able to haul himself out of there, but one step wrong and the hole would collapse.

Presley was out there, running for his life.

Tom had to save him.

But one chance was all he had.

CHAPTER

33

WITH A TWITCH, TOM grabbed the edge of a stone in front of him. His range of motion was too limited for him to stretch out his arms properly. He had to turn and twist his body at different angles to even be able to move a tiny amount. The stone he held stuck out of the soil wall at the same height as his shoulders. How much weight could it hold? He tried to peer up at the inky sky again, but the rain continued to beat against his face and forced him to lower his sight. It would be a challenge to get out of there, but he couldn't leave Presley. The dog meant more to him than his own life. He couldn't disappoint and abandon either Presley or Margaret. Without them, his life would be over.

Tom swallowed hard, and the wounds that covered his body pulsed and burned. He wiggled the stone with both of his hands. What if it didn't hold? He closed his eyes for a second. If he didn't climb up, he would die down there, a slow and painful death, all alone in the darkness.

Like you deserve, trucker!

The voice made him shudder.

Stay with us down here, Tommie! Don't you dare leave!

Tom swallowed hard. Even if the stone held his weight, would he have the strength to climb up to the leash above? It couldn't be more than a few feet to the leash, but he couldn't afford any mistakes now.

He opened his eyes and searched for a way up. How far could it be? Ten feet? Fifteen?

You'll never get up!

You're weak!

Tom pressed his right boot into the wall in front of him and grimaced. The wall's cold surface made his foot pulsate in its grasp. While his left boot hung against the darkness, he used his right leg to push himself upward a few inches. It wasn't much, but it helped. He pushed his left foot into the soil wall and searched for more stones to grab. Another pull, a few more inches. When he was about to pull on a third stone, his fingers slid along the jagged edge, and his pulse increased in his throat. He dropped his grip for a second, pressed his back against the wall behind him, and managed to get a new grip on another stone. His fingers turned white. The rain made everything slippery, like an eel in water.

Underneath him, the darkness disappeared into empty space.

He was on his way up for real. It was him versus nature. It hadn't killed him yet, and he wouldn't give up trying to survive.

In the air, with his fingers on the wet stone, his muscles burned down his arms and all the way back towards his shoulders. He tried to turn his face to the sky above, but the rain continued to whip him in the eyes. He had to guess where to put his hands. He trembled, feeling with his palms, one at the time, above him. When he found another stone, he pulled himself higher, and a sharpened rock dug into his chest like the tip of an arrow. He couldn't help but let out a grunt. He closed his eyes, grimaced, and continued to push. The stone pressed deeper into his skin, and his hands shook in protest. This time, there was nothing he could grab. Despite his stinging muscles, he stretched out his arms, unsure how far he had come, and tried to reach the leash. He couldn't. It was still dangling up there somewhere.

The taste of iron grew stronger in his mouth. He spat blood-mixed saliva down through the darkness and fed whatever lived below. A voice drifted back to him.

You can't do it!

Tom closed his eyes and his pulse banged harder in his ears.

He twisted even more and managed to grip another slippery stone on the other side. A crunching sound appeared.

He didn't have much time.

Let go!

Tom grimaced and tried to block out the voice.

He worked with his legs and managed to place his left boot on a stone farther up. But with a hollow sound, the stone broke out from the wall, and his body hung loose inside the hole while his pulsating fingers were all that saved him from falling. His eyes widened in panic, spinning like an old windmill about to break. He tried to grab at the wall with his boots, but they slipped off as if covered in bacon grease. Shocking pain exploded up his left leg and radiated all the way to his lower back. He couldn't hold much longer.

Release the grip!

Tom shook as he glanced down to see if he could put his feet somewhere, but everything was pitch black. A claustrophobic and gruesome thought washed over him. The rain would sooner or later make him lose his grip, and he would plummet to his death. Desperation kicking in, he pulled himself upward with a grim scream, while he scratched with his boots along the walls. His body wracked with pain, his back like a rotten flank of meat, a minimum load would crush him at this point. But the thought of being stuck down there forever sent shivers all the way into his marrow. He stretched his arms to their limit, and, to his surprise, he touched the ledge. It had been hidden by a layer of tangled roots, which had twisted themselves into the walls. The roots were thin and would tear apart with any added weight.

You're weak.

"Shut up!" Tom contorted his body until an icy feeling slipped into his spine. He couldn't afford to fail now. He jumped up toward the leash, hand outstretched, and grabbed at it. But it was stuck. He gripped the twisted root in panic and tried to tear the leash free without result. Instead, the roots cut their way deep into his right palm, like barbed wire, and warmth dripped down his arm. His entire body weight was being supported by a single root, which he held with one hand now, while he swatted with the other at the leash. The spindly root gave off a ripping sound, like a shirt caught on a nail. The tearing noise was absorbed by the walls.

It's over!
His eyes went wide.
You're worthless, Tommie!
If he ever wanted to get out of the hole, he had to do better.
Now, it was just a matter of seconds.

CHAPTER

34

TOM RELEASED THE LEASH and gripped another root next to the first one, and his other palm split open. More blood snaked down his arm. As he hung there in the air, he stared at his big, mangled worker hands, with large blood vessels resembling rivers on a map. For fifteen years, Margaret had pointed out he had hands big as catcher's mitts, but he never gave it a thought until now, when he was facing death. Not only did they look big, they looked damn clumsy. But they were strong.

You're weak!

Tom squeezed the roots together and screamed.

A sudden crack from the wall pulled him down, and his heart jumped up against his throat. The bursting sound from the roots continued deeper inside the wall.

Tom uttered a low grunt, gritted his teeth, and tensed his pulsating muscles.

Let go! Your dog is already dead!

The panic swarmed through his body, and he became dizzy.

A distant and isolated noise caught his attention.

One bark.

Two barks.

His beloved Presley was alive—and he was somewhere close by.

A glow ignited inside Tom and awakened his mind to a higher level. More adrenaline now poured into his body in gushing waves.

No, Tom! You don't get it, do you? Your dog is dead! He's been dead since the crash! He's already rotting in the ground!

"No!" Tom swung his body and managed to get some support with his boots on the wall. Soil crumbled down and, together with the blood that dripped from his arms, fell into the nothingness below. The roots stretched, threatening to give way.

Tom took all the power he had left in his body and pulled himself closer to the edge. There wasn't much left to go, but the roots cut deeper into his flesh and made his eyes blur with tears of pain.

You can't escape from here! You're stuck here, like everyone else!

He pulled, adjusted his grip, and forced his body upward. His fingers throbbed and turned white, as he grabbed a hold of the undergrowth on the edge of hole.

With a shredding sound, another root gave up, and the dirt began to collapse around him, as a stone struck between his shoulders and knocked the air from his lungs. His adrenaline crossed the border into shock. Sweat sprayed from him. But he gripped the edge.

It's over!

Tom glanced down the hole. His pulse bounced inside him. He could release his grip and everything would be finished. He wouldn't have to suffer anymore.

What are you waiting for? There is no point trying! Let go!

Presley barked again from somewhere in the forest, now deeper and several in succession.

Tom clenched his teeth. The darkness wanted to swallow him, but he couldn't allow it. He grabbed another root with his bloody right hand and pulled.

More barks, together with a light shrill.

The dog isn't real!

Tom let out a crazed scream and continued to pull himself upward. He yanked himself toward the opening. No matter how much his hands now burned, and how much his muscles cramped in his body, he continued pulling.

Let go! You aren't strong enough!

Tom tried to quiet the words, but they echoed inside his head. No, he couldn't let them decide. He grimaced, pulled his bloody forearms over the edge into the fresh air, and when he managed to get his chest over, his ribs protested under his weight. His legs now dangled inside the still darkness of the hole, and without either light or hope in the waiting room of death, Tom Richards struggled forward, crawling his way along the bushes that lined the ground in front of him. As he continued to grab and pull at the shrubs, their spikes stuck him in his face and pulled at his clothes.

He gathered his last bit of power and drug himself across the ground and out of the hell hole. He rolled onto his back and took a deep breath; the rain splattered against him. His whole body consisted of nothing but a lump of pain. But even though his body was ready to give out, he couldn't stay there.

He had to find Presley.

The moment he scrambled to his feet, another bark came.

West.

Tom staggered through the unharvested plant kingdom toward the barks.

CHAPTER

35

TOM'S HAPPINESS AND GRATITUDE for escaping the Devil's dungeon slid away, as the recurring sound of Presley's bark was drowned out by his dark, irrational thoughts that were couched in painful despair. A mixture of desire and prolonged imprisonment in a narrow tunnel of misery nearly squelched his ability to continue. He had no idea what to do when he arrived. The Devil was still out there somewhere.

What are you doing, trucker? Crawl back to the hole!

Tom pressed his hands against his skull.

The wind threw a delightful scent of autumnal sovereignty against him, which provoked tears of euphoria, and in the brilliance of autumn colors, despite the afflictions on his body, a sensation of welcome overcame him. But the uncertainty of misery still lingered. His limbs ached, and the throbbing sensitivity broke his ability to rely on his own belief. What if he were searching in the wrong direction? The rain against his already cold body made him shiver even more. The forest was still the same, with its colorful pallet of nature. The trees still swayed toward him, while his head pounded in the same rhythm as his heartbeats. He continued onward, until something in the wind's grace pulled him out of this false beauty and security and gave rise to an indecision that made his body stiffen.

Darkness crept closer.

More barks sounded nearby.

Tom stopped and turned. Those barks sounded more feral. They sailed out over the forest then came to an abrupt stop.

CHAPTER

36

THE TEMPERATURE SANK, AND the world still continued its natural jargon. But for Tom Richards, everything had stopped, and the darkness that slowly crept over him wanted him dead. As the rain had decreased to a drizzle, he continued to drag his body through the fate of the God-forgotten plains and valleys as if he had been filled with an inner determination that couldn't be extinguished with ordinary trials, but which fed on the deliberate expansion of hope for recovering the dog. After Presley's last shrilling scream, the dog's barks had ceased. But Tom had found him once already, and he would find him again. He had stuffed the leash in his pocket, and would use it when the right time came. Only a slash of light remained in the sky above, and his search among the ferocious thickets and storm-worn pines was pushing him to the edge of collapse.

Don't you hear me, trucker? Your dog is dead! Dead!

"No," Tom whispered.

Presley's barks had been close yet still far away, like a confusion of rumbling between the atmosphere and the mountain chain. Without any more tips to follow, he was unsure where to search next. Presley could be anywhere, dead or alive, and the thought made his stomach turn.

A couple of days earlier, Tom had considered himself a man of rational logic. He had never believed in legends like Bigfoot, the Loch Ness Monster, and all the other bullshit humans made up to explain their fears. But what George Goldman had told him back by the restaurant had sowed a seed inside him. When the Devil had appeared in the cave, Tom's understanding of rationality had imploded. If the Devil was real, maybe the rest of the world's evil forces were as well.

The real danger and evil in the world had earlier, for Tom, been locked behind doors and in cells. Except for the obvious violence that spread over the world, there were also plagues of terror hidden from the public in forms of poison and weapons, blood that sprawled in revolutions, and ruthless attacks that started full-scale wars. It all happened in secret. Everybody knew about it, but at the same time they knew nothing of its ferocity. Evil had perpetrated time. Stories had survived through centuries, transferred from generation to generation in contagion. Some stories had lasted longer than they were supposed to. Fear and fascination. It was among the cruel folklore of local stories where wickedness and evil sought their advantage. Children could point out witches who, in ruthless fervor, were burned at the stake without explanation. But even though most of the children had a tendency to accept what most adults considered madness, in the form of fantasies, they still had power to deal with evil. It was often in the temporary imagination where every idea was developed. But it wasn't the children who carried out the *real* evil; it was the ones who accepted their stories without any serious afterthought. It was the adults who, instead of taking responsibility for the difficulties and trials of life, became convinced of the power of evil, with minds too weak to realize acceptance before fear. Evil was as easy to develop as love.

Tom scratched his head. The desperation for Presley had now led him into a darker place that made his skin crawl. Nature eyed him. He wanted to shout at the wicked world, curse it for what had happened, but since nobody could hear him, it would be a waste of energy. Instead, he kicked at a stone to release his frustration, and in the same moment something caught his eye.

Something lay in the grass a few feet away. Something that didn't move.

CHAPTER

37

THERE IS NO ROOM to believe the creations of the world enabled a sensible appearance. When Tom Richards found Presley under a fallen tree trunk, next to some trampled ferns, he almost collapsed at the sight.

The back of the dog in front of him didn't move, but it sure was Presley, with his golden colored hair. Dirt and blood were matted in the fur.

Tom's legs trembled, and his eyes filled with tears. The sight made him nauseous, and acid pushed up through his throat. He fell down on his knees and tried to vomit, but nothing came. He instead gasped for his breath, and in that moment, it was like his soul was pulled out of his body.

Presley didn't move at all.

Tom held his breath and stumbled to the dog.

He grabbed the wet and bloodied fur ready to face his nightmare, but Presley cracked out a whine, and Tom's breath escaped in a gasp of relief.

Presley wriggled with nerves. The dog had been trying to hide, and Tom had scared him.

Tom embraced his dog and cried out. "You're *alive,* buddy!"

But something wasn't right.

38

IT HAD BEEN YEARS since Tom squeezed his dog as tight as he now did. Despite the cold, his body was filled with an inner heat of the feelings he had buried inside him. His tears dripped to the ground, and if he could, he would never release the dog again. Love flowed through him like a river. He kissed Presley on his head, patted him for comfort, and put the leash on him for security. Together, they would get away from here as fast as they could. He would never let Presley disappear again.

But where did all the blood come from?

The dog didn't have any wounds or even scratches. For the moment, it didn't matter. All Tom wanted, was to get out of there. With Presley by his side, they moved together over fallen branches and deeper into the unknown. There had to be a way out. Even mazes had exits. But in a maze, a man could at least follow a path.

Tom leaned against a tree and stared into the forest with wide eyes. The Devil still lurked out there, and it would just be a matter of time before their paths crossed again. But Tom knew his duty. He had to do what the higher powers wanted him to do from the beginning. He had to kill the Devil before the Devil killed them both. It was the only way to survive.

Darkness continued its slow creep.

As Tom and Presley made their way through the forest, whispers came from the overgrowth that hid its dark secrets.

You can't hide, Tom.

The voices mixed with the light sound of the drizzling rain splatting against tree trunks and bushes. They came in different tones making themselves known, like icy fingers against his skin.

He's watching you!

Tom snarled. They continued forward along an unharvested terrain with multicolored flowers that spit out their sweet smells.

There must be an end to this wretched forest *somewhere.* They needed to get to the road and away from this obsidian terror.

A deep, distanced sound came on the whistling wind, like a strike to a bass drum.

Tom stopped and turned.

A droning, electric, out-of-tune guitar joined the drumming, and bass chords kicked in.

Tom frowned, and his skin prickled. He glanced at Presley, jaw dropped in surprise. Music? He looked into the trees behind him, and the sound disappeared. But something else appeared. It was a whisper, and it came from a tree close by.

Tom walked toward it. Inside the tree was a hole, not bigger than a golf ball. He put his left ear against the tree, and a creaky voice said: *"Hey! Why don't you kill yourself, Tommie?"*

Tom jumped back and fell on his ass, eyes wide.

He pulled the leash tighter, and Presley rubbed against him.

"Let's get out of here," Tom sobbed and rose from the ground with his eyes still on the trees. "Before something else happens."

CHAPTER

39

IN THE TREES AND mountains of the Dalton Highway area, the normal world ceased to exist, and loneliness became a part of survival. The evil forces, which had earlier only revealed themselves at night, now roamed during the day, an ever-present discomfort, which stung inside Tom's stomach like the tip of a sharp knife poking at his entrails. The immoral wickedness no longer needed the safety of the dark shadows. The world Tom once had known as genuine and true, no longer existed. It was now a made-up empire of lies and turbid secrets. This Alaska Tom now found himself in, didn't contain the same Alaska he had grown up in. The wild landscape he used to approach with splendor, with its colorful shiftings, from pink to golden yellow, from streaks of red to deep smudges of green, now concealed an unnatural darkness along the undiscovered area. Alaska had always been the state where a man could dig gold and search in rocky grounds for oil, and where a man could find old hunters who told folk-stories down at the local bar, where wooden walls were covered with animal trophies, such as furs, heads, and horns, and where local beer was offered in its finest quality. For Tom, Alaska had, for a long time, been the discoverer's journey, filled with adventures at the farthest, foggy tundras and glittering fjords, snow-catching glaciers and exciting safari trips, a revelation that could last for days while hiking trails in famous wilderness areas, but now, it also contained a mysterious power, a bleak, obscure reality where nothing was what it seemed to be. Normally, nothing would be able to stop the average, adventurous man from exploring the state, nor the local hunters from grilling their freshly caught salmon at an open fire, while the sight of the paddle steamer passed over in front of the glittering snow-capped mountain peaks, and a crimson sunset fell asleep behind. But man could no longer trust the Alaskan wilderness. Even in the most beautiful places, a putrid hate, together with the undiscovered truth, hid in the shadows.

Those last days, Tom's understanding of the world had shifted from worrying about debts, to a fragmented understanding of structure and logic when it came to survival. He stood alone against the evil side of nature. The Alaska he now faced erased all his years of delight and majesty and replaced it with a cavern of secrets and lies. It tore all rationality from his mind.

Tom and Presley now stopped next to an overgrown bush. Nature stood quiet, while the rain subsided even more. A silent breeze pulled through the trees, and a group of ravens shrieked overhead. It could have been any old day, but the Devil still lurked out there, *waiting*.

You're nothing, trucker!

Tom plopped to the grass and breathed deep. Presley fell down beside him and panted. Leaves, sticks, and smeared berries were tangled in the dog's fur, and the rain made him look older.

But it was something about this particular forest, that neither looked nor behaved like any other forest in Alaska, and it chilled his insides. The forest around Dalton Highway seemed to reverse the laws of nature.

Drowsy and emaciated, Tom leaned back against a stone, as his temples pulsed a painful pace. Each throb of misery moved further into his body, and he let out a whine. The nausea had come and gone since the crash, but now it seem to take root in his guts, and it gave him a want to vomit. But he couldn't. He needed more water. But from where? His thoughts were thick as batter. He needed caffeine. For such a caffeine-dependent drinker like him, he needed his dose of coffee— up to five cups a day. If he didn't get it, bolts of pain in his head increased like the tightening of a vice.

Tom glanced at the tired dog next to him. Presley needed to rest, and Tom did too. His eyes eyelids were heavy. Just a *little* rest. They were covered among the shadows, and hanging branches, so now seemed like a good time. He leaned his aching back to the angular stone, covered in greenish, slick moss, and closed his eyes for a moment. He sat still, blocked out the sounds around him, and abandoned his thoughts of the cold, dank forest. He thought of a warm bed. But in his mind, he didn't lay in his and Margaret's bed; instead, he lay in his childhood bed, where his father once boxed his ears so hard, he had to stay home from school for a week to wait for the swelling to go down.

He imagined himself in pajamas reading a comic book. A poster of Jimi Hendrix hung next to the window (and it often flattered when someone opened the door). The fresh scent of Paco Rabanne Pour Homme cologne he had received from his mother as a Christmas gift two years earlier, when he was ten, swirled in the room. On his left stood his wooden desk, where he had some issues of *Stardom* magazine. He took them from his mother, when she had finished them, and painted in them. By the magazines was a stack of drawing paper (and dozens of assorted colored pencils), together with a Rubik's Cube and an empty Connect Four: his favorites. But it wasn't often someone wanted to play games with him. Tom didn't have many friends, not more than *her*, his so-called imaginary friend. But she was real. She had always been real to him. But his mother thought differently. It had been her idea to visit Miss Paterson, thinking his imaginary friend was an effect due to the death of his father. But it wasn't.

On the floor below, on a dirty car mat with crumpled corners, stood a couple of Starsky & Hutch-cars he also had received as a Christmas present some years back. His muddy skateboard, with a lightning bolt painted on the underside of it, leaned against the wall. By the door, stood a bookshelf filled with comics. As a child he read anything he got his hands on.

But something wasn't right in the scene.

One part of him wanted to continue to study his old room, to fall into a deep sleep and take comfort in his childhood memories, where he, for the moment, could relax, but an anxiety crept inside him and stole his breath. Something hid in the darkness.

And it stared at him.

Who's there, Tommie? Who's watching?

A hollow buzzing tore Tom out of his daydreams. He stared into the forest. The wind blew against the burgeoning pines in front of him. Nothing was close enough to make that kind of noise. He must have dozed off. To ignorant eyes, the forest might still have looked like a calm and beautiful piece of nature, but things out there were different.

But then, puzzled by the sound, Tom turned to Presley and pulled the leash with a twist. "You heard it too, buddy?"

The dog sighed.

Tom calmed himself and tried to get his legs working. There had been a period in his life, when he still lived in the city, and spent his mornings jogging around the district area near the park, when he could run a mile with ease. It was hard for him to just sit in the truck without doing anything those days. But over the years, he had become unrecognizable to his previous self. The energy had disappeared, and the depression made it worse. The bills. The fights.

The same noise sounded. The metallic buzz made him think a failing industrial fan was hidden somewhere in the forest, which helped to push the clouds forward.

What the hell was it?

The uncertainty, and Tom's own curiosity, forced him the rest of the way to his feet. He pulled the leash. "Come on, buddy. It's coming from this way. We have to move. Now!"

They followed the sound through the tangled weeds.

Gray clouds split, and Tom and Presley found themselves surrounded by mountain peaks, hovering like hungry animals waiting for their prey. The wind was weak and the humidity collected on Tom's upper lip.

Far beyond the forest, the mechanical noise continued to emerge. The sound became clearer and sharper as if it came *closer*.

Tom looked toward the sky.

The sound seeped through the clouds of the rainy gray sky. Where did it come from?

Tom and Presley moved farther over the terrain, as Tom's lungs squeezed out a wheeze.

The sound came closer.

As they emerged from another cluster of pine trees, the silhouette of a dark helicopter appeared in the sky. It moved along the treetops, the steady sound of its rotating blades chopping through the wind.

CHAPTER

40

TOM THREW THE LEASH on the ground and waved at the sky as if he were on fire, but nothing came out of his mouth. The adrenaline pumped through his body and everything went in slow motion. He turned to Presley, and uncontrollable tears ran down his cheeks. When he faced the helicopter again, it dipped to the side, flew over the treetops, and disappeared.

"No," Tom whispered. "*No!*"

He fell down on his knees, facing the swaying tree tops. "What have I done?"

You think they're looking for you, trucker? Never. They don't care about you! They want you dead!

What was the truth? If the helicopter was searching for them, maybe the crew would have seen him and Presley earlier? They'd been out there for a long time. Something wasn't right. No, something wasn't right at all.

You're stuck here, trucker! Stuck!

Tom frowned, got up, took up the leash again, and pulled the dog closer to him. He and Presley had to seek cover. Or should he run after the helicopter?

They don't need you!

Tom gasped for breath, unsure what to do. In panic, he ducked behind a big stone and pulled Presley into his arms. He couldn't risk it. Sweat bursted out of every pore on his body. He stunk like he hadn't showered in a month. He snorted out a single, nervous laugh. What the hell was he thinking? The pilots couldn't be trusted. Could they? What if somebody had sent the helicopter to monitor their trek in the wild, like they were on one of those reality TV shows?

They want you dead! Don't you get that?

"We can't trust them," Tom whispered to Presley. "We can't fucking trust *them,* either."

The dog whined a short one, and Tom couldn't control crying out. He ran his hand through his greasy hair, and his cry turned into another burst of laughter. His mind raced. What was he supposed to do? What the hell was the pilot's visit supposed to mean? They wanted to see if he was still alive. They wanted to see if he had finished his job. But they must have seen the Devil somewhere close, and understood the work wasn't finished. Would they make Margaret suffer instead?

Tom tried to breath. He had to get home and warn Margaret before it was too late. What if they put *her* out here for some kind of experiment?

Tom clenched his jaw.

No.

Nothing could ever happen to her. She was his only love; his woman, soulmate, best friend, living dream, and ... *enemy?* She knew *everything* about him... Could it be ... *her?* Could she have planned this? Had *she* orchestrated the crash? Was she the reason he was lost in the wilderness? Tom breathed heavily. Could it be that he would die in the forest and she would get the house? Was that what she wanted all along? Had she traded his life for the damned *house?*

Tom took another deep breath and raked his hands through his hair over and over again. Had she met someone else? What did she actually do when she went to her mother? Did she no longer love him? Could she have left him for some *rich* man? For someone who could take care of her in a way Tom couldn't? Did she do all this together with... her *mother?* Had *they* ...

Tom released Presley from his grip. The dog relaxed in the grass next to him, but with his eyes wide open.

What the hell was Margaret thinking? And what was it she wanted to tell him when he came home? Could it be that she had left him for another man? Could it be that ... he laughed at an unthinkable truth which, despite limited opportunity, was nevertheless reasonable... could she be *pregnant*? If so ... *who* was the father?

She doesn't love you anymore!

Tom pulled out the cigarette pack from his chest pocket, fumbled out a smoke, and put it between his scabby lips. The taste of iron struck inside his mouth. The cigarette was covered in blood. He looked down at his hands where his palms were cut open. The blood had coagulated on parts of the wounds and left a series of clotted black streaks, but some of the areas still seeped scarlet.

He took out the lighter, jerked back the sparking-wheel with his thumb, and pushed down. A sparkle of faint blue flashed up and turned into a flaming glow. He held his left hand over the flame, and the heat made the wound pulse.

He laughed, yanked the lighter away, and set the cigarette on fire. With a long inhalation, the smoke filled his lungs, and the taste of tobacco mixed with iron made him cringe.

Disgusting.

He could throw away the cigarette for the bad taste, but he only had one left. Where had he seen that last gas station? It couldn't be too far. His head pulsed. He needed to sleep. But not now.

Tom looked around as if a station might materialize. He needed cigarettes, but his thoughts jumped to who that bitch could have met behind his back. Could it be that damned doctor, Fredriech? Or had her mother helped her find someone?

Another inhalation. A deep one. His lungs spasmed.

"Don't worry, buddy," Tom said and turned to Presley. "They won't see the smoke from here, anyway. They don't know we're here. Got it? They *never* will. We are smarter than them, buddy. Trust me."

He flicked the lighter once again and smiled at the flame fluttering back and forth in the power of the wind. Then he blew out the flame and closed his eyes.

Maybe Margaret was after his life insurance policy. Perhaps she could no longer stand the pressure of not being able to pay off all the debts ... To live with bills had never been her goal in life. She *demanded* richness. She didn't want a damn loser who couldn't pay his own bills, like Tom. But he had always done what he could—as *any* man would do for his wife. She was his everything and he loved her. But what had changed?

You've always been a worthless man!

Tom smiled wider as he stared into the colorful flame of the fire. How dare she go so far for money? She would regret it. In time, she would regret it. And she could forget about getting any insurance money, or save the house. Tom would show her who had the power. She could've asked for a simple divorce, but, no, the death of Tom would be better. It would make *her* the victim, the one everybody would feel sorry for. The fact it would make her single, wouldn't bother her. And it could give her time to play the grieving widow. But not if she'd already met another man. A man she wanted a child with.

A wry laugh burst from Tom's chest.

Would her family and friends flood her phone with impersonal texts like, "We're so very sorry!" and "Our thoughts are with you!" How many flowers would she get after his so-called accident? Flowers that would rot, like the news about Tom's death and how Margaret had lost her *beloved* soul mate. Bullshit. She had always been *his* soulmate. Until *now.* Now she could go to hell and rot in her grave. How could she go behind his back like this? But she couldn't have done all this on her own. Margaret was a wise woman, but not *that* wise. She must have had help. It must have been that damned lover, whoever he was, or her mother.

Tom laughed again and stared into the forest. How long had she been planning this?

Margaret didn't have a poker face, everyone who knew her, knew that. Did she really want Tom to be on one of those bulletin boards at the rest area? Would *anybody* even bother putting up a picture of him? Who would even care about his death? He didn't have any friends left, and soon he wouldn't have a wife either.

Why don't you kill yourself, Tom? End it, just like your father did!

Tom closed his eyes. "No, *shut* up!"

Margaret doesn't want you!

Tom would show her. He would show Margaret. The truth prickled his insides, gnawed through his flesh and bones, and made him laugh at himself for everything that had happened. Would the imaginative sadness make his wife happy, and would she take pills to cover her happiness? She could ask the doctor for something addictive, like the doctor's own cock shoved up right in her ass.

She's already spreading those legs, Tommie! Don't you get it? She's fucking someone right now! She can't stand you any longer. She doesn't love you! She never has! She hates you!

Tom couldn't believe what was happening. "No," he whispered. Wouldn't she miss him after all they'd been through? Everything he had done for her? Would she really be happy to lose him, or would she stand at the kitchen window from morning to evening, as the wrinkles grew stronger and broader along her face, until she, one day, woke up and realized what she had done? Or would she fall into the land of dreams every night without even giving a thought about what had happened to her husband out there in the wild?

She knows it all, and she loves it.

If anyone knew Margaret's limits, it was Tom. If he knew her *right*, she would, after his so-called-death, drain her sadness by taking someone home from the pub, some snob who invited her to drinks and sympathized with her grief but who wanted to get in her panties. If she hadn't hooked up with that doctor yet, then maybe it was someone she knew from before. But what stabbed at Tom's heart like a knife tip, was the fact that she would fuck other men after he died. It would be the worst betrayal of all. That damned pub night would lead to more: a morning coffee, a good chat, some kisses. How long would it take before all their wedding photos disappeared from the walls? Would all their memories get tossed in the cold, dusty cellar, among the dirty floors and broken cobwebs in the roof corners, abandoned, almost like Tom found himself in right now? Would he become a memory that faded away with time?

No.

He couldn't lose himself like that. He had a home to go back to. He and Presley had a life to continue. If Margaret wanted a divorce, she would get it. If Tom had to kill someone on the road for it, he would do so without thinking twice, even if it was the Devil himself.

Tom stubbed the cigarette against his boot, threw it away, and squeezed Presley to him.

How would things turn out if he came home after all? How would Margaret react? She would regret it.

Tom smiled again, that same wry grimace.

You worthless trucker! Look at you! Look at what you've become! You're nothing.

But Tom continued smiling.

Whatever happened, he had to get home. But first, he had something important to do.

He touched the lighter and couldn't help but laugh.

He had an idea, and this time, he wouldn't fail.

CHAPTER

41

TOM SIGHTED OUT ALONG the trees in front of him. Nature concealed any exits. But there *had* to be a way out of there. A way back to his truck. Without the truck, everything was doomed, and his plan would fail.

He laughed. He needed a drink. A big, strong drink to make him forget about what lurked out there. The idea of alcohol caused his tongue to ripple in waves. Any sort of liquid would be good right now, but alcohol had always been his medicine against all the pain and broken emotions of life. The alcohol had, at times, helped him out with fragile attempts of fictional rescue, where the possibility of balance existed inside the bottle. At least that is what he had convinced himself to believe over the years. The alcohol had never been a *real* rescue, instead, it had become another barrier, which gave rise to a more problematic task—coping with life. He couldn't get away from the fact that much of the money he put aside, instead, got used to diffuse feelings of incompletion. It had never been a secret that he used alcohol to conceal his meaningless influence.

Tom put his hands on his head as if it would improve his thoughts. From which way had he originally come? Which mountain had he met the Devil in? He turned around and tried to remember, but all his mind could register was how the trees around him were standing around him like a group of bullies. They were mocking him for his incompetence, for not being able to find his way back, for not being a *real* man.

You better give up, Tom.

"What do you want from me?" Tom shouted and swung a fist against a tree trunk. "I've nothing to give *any* of you!"

Don't you understand? It's over.

More pain shot through his head. This time, it was an ongoing surge inside him, with the sound of thousands of different voices, like a flock of screeching birds. Thoughts flowed through him and drowned in each other like waves hitting the shore. Female voices, children's voices, even the occasional man's voice. They all came and tried to outdo each other their sharp shouting to a point where Tom stuffed his knuckles in his ears to make them stop. His limit had been reached a long time ago, and the voices needed to beat it. He pushed his knuckles harder, trying to press the noise from his consciousness.

Nothing happened.

The intensity crept through his head, farther down through his body, and he fell to the ground while a scream escaped his mouth as uncontrolled as a hiccup. "Please," he begged. "Leave me alone!"

No one listened.

Some of the voices spoke directly to him, while others chatted with each other in a buzzing babble, like a swarm of wasps.

We have to talk, Tom.

Don't you understand who we are?

He's nothing but a worthless little boy.

His headache pulsated in a rhythmic slam. The worst voices were the whisperers.

He's waiting for you... just around the corner... Why don't you go and see, Tom?

Their sound was low and constant.

You'll never find a way out of here.

Tom clenched his right fist and hit himself straight in the forehead. One time. Two times. Three.

Your wife wants you dead, Tom Richards.

He continued to punch himself until a pressure released within him, but the rhythmic pulse still kept time in his head, now bouncing in pain. The voices disappeared one after the other in a low murmur, but the burst of agony doubled his vision momentarily until reality pulled him back into the picture of growling trees. His eyes were filled with tears, and there wasn't much left to Tom's rational way of thinking.

Presley watched him from the side and breathed a heavy sigh.

Even though the world had quieted for Tom, he still hadn't found a way out of there. But he had an idea. A vicious and ruthless thought that could only be fulfilled through a masterful revenge.

But he still needed the truck.

CHAPTER

42

TOGETHER, TOM AND PRESLEY headed north. The grey and gloomy sky broke open and exploded with a thunder clap. There couldn't be more than an hour left before real darkness would fill the whole country and make the moon into a golden-colored doorknob floating in an obscure infinity.

They had to hurry.

Tom's head still pulsed and made him tired, as if termites were tearing at him from the inside out.

The rain made him shiver and with every footstep, it got soaked in his boots. He had lost feeling in both his feet in the last couple of hours. He couldn't tell if his feet were blistered or covered in athlete's foot or worse. But he continued walking. Once in a while, his toes throbbed— maybe that was a good sign.

Tom hunched over as he moved along the wet grass. He wondered how far it was back to the truck. How long would it take to get there? If he couldn't find it before the night crept closer, it would be over. There was no one to help him. No one he could trust. If he wanted to get away from there, he had to trust *himself* and himself only.

Why don't you stop trying, trucker? It's over.

No.

He couldn't give up. He stepped forward, and everything looked the same. *There's no point, trucker! You're stuck here!*

Tom pulled the leash and Presley followed. His arms were covered in tiny scratches from all the thorny bushes he had passed. They resembled a set of secret hieroglyphics from some ancient ritual as if they tried to tell him something.

A group of birds passed through the rainclouds and screamed. Tom looked up and stiffened. It was more of those bristle-thighed curlews. What George Goldman had said back by the restaurant, now came to him with a sudden knock. The old man had explained to him how the birds migrated southwest around now. Tom tried to think, tried to focus. Where had he been driving? Where had he crashed? Which direction had he, for the first time, searched after Presley in? His ability to search through the memory box seemed out of reach. The birds would take him to the road. If he managed to come to the road, he could finish what he had planned.

Don't you trust the birds, you maniac!

Tom and Presley followed the same directions as the birds, until they reached a downward sloping hill covered in frozen ferns, stumps, and molted feathers. The bottom collapsed into a barren field. Tom picked up the pace, despite his heavy clothes, which were soaked by the rain, searching for the road. His boots gave off a damp, squishy sound with every step, and his feet ached more than ever.

Overhead, the birds had disappeared. But Tom and Presley had followed their directions through ferns, moss-covered trees, withered flowers, and wild weeds without finding the road.

There's no road out here! It never has been! Don't you get that, trucker? You're a fool for thinking something else! You're stuck here, stuck like everybody else!

The hazy light turned the trees into gray shadow dancers. Either it had become brighter from the rising moonlight, or Tom's eyes had gotten used to the already scarce illumination. Whatever the reason, it was easier to see.

The truck is gone!

A distant humming sound slipped its way through the forest. Tom stopped for a moment, darting glances in all directions. To anyone else, the place, regardless of the season, appeared a delightful paradise, but for those who knew better, the place was a god-forgotten platform for nature's atrocities and bestial history. He hurried under an overgrown tree, whose leaves hung like sleeping bats above him. Some of those bat-leaves stuck in the dog's fur. On the other side of the trees, stood a place of colorful plants and picturesque country flowers, while the ground a bit above it, turned into a kind of green-covered area with an overgrown plateau of views beyond the winding *highway* below.

And without a warning, the road appeared right in front of them, as if it had been right there all along.

Tom's eyes followed the road, while his mind ordered him to flee down there. The sound of the truck had been real. But he couldn't give in to rescue.

Not yet.

"We can do it," he told Presley. "But we have to wait."

The dog looked at him with heavy panting, and with a fur filled with blood and dirt, he laid down and began to lick his paws with a low growl.

Tom waited until the truck passed, and then moved over the caribou-trampled ground, stumbling on stones and crushing insects under his soggy boots. A herd of grey caribou-stretched a few hundred feet down, like melting ice, and the night sky crept closer.

Presley came after, limping.

There wasn't much time left. And Tom only had one chance to kill the Devil. This was his chance to save the world, and his own freedom.

CHAPTER

43

TOM RICHARDS AND PRESLEY escaped the forest late on Saturday afternoon, the same time a chilling breeze pushing the afternoon sun behind the mountains. The golden moon now hovered above as a group of ravens made their presence known, like a swarm of fat wasps. The rain ceased, and the sky held only a few thin wisps of clouds off in the distance. The whole of Alaska was on its way to being engulfed in the night, but the moonlight kept on. How much longer would it light their way? They needed to find the truck. One more night out there would kill them both.

The road in front of them was lumpy and covered with loose gravel. It hooked to the right behind a group of tall trees.

Tom was lost, frozen, and hungry, and every cell in his body screamed in pain. Emptiness and degradation filled his body, almost like a living death. Sweat seeped from every pore. His eyes blurred everything into a smudge. But if he could pull off his plan, everything would soon be back to normal, and what they'd been through would be nothing but a stupid memory.

Presley came behind him, still lumping, still panting.

The trees swayed over the road and lulled Tom deeper into his brain-weary trance. Tears ran down his face, pelting the ground with his salty discharge. Like the flick of a light switch, the past two days played out in his mind. Memories of how he had left home with Presley, the fight with Margaret over the phone, the red car by the road, the gas station, the missing people on the bulletin boards, George Goldman, the restaurant, and even the crash.

The images pulsated inside his skull.

You'll never get out of here.

This road won't take you anywhere.

Tom closed his eyes for a second, and when he opened them again, he focused on the trees, which reached toward heaven. Everything snapped into a sharp focus. It had to be somewhere close by he had lost control. He couldn't have gone that far from the crash site. But where had he crashed?

He threw his gaze to the ditches in search of any tread marks. The grass was matted in a spray of conflicting directions. Darkness was overcoming the moon, deadening his chances of seeing much else. Except for the truck, he also needed water and food. But he had it all in the truck.

A crackling sound shot from the forest, and he quickened his pace.

A few ravens flew over the treetops and shrieked a hoarse warning.

Tom's legs burned with fatigue. He *had* to be close. Where could that fucking truck be?

There is no truck, Tom! Haven't you figured that out, yet?It's gone!

"Shut up" Tom shouted and yanked on his clumpy hair.

You're fooling yourself, trucker!

The raggedy duo walked for about twenty minutes more before they came to a place where the grass had been chewed and mauled by something big. Farther down the ditch, the bushes were smashed to bits. Tom's senses were overcome with the confusion of sights and smells, and for a minute, he thought he was in his own garden. The scent of jasmine flowers and buttery apples blended with the bitter, but prominent, smell of engine oil and gasoline.

Don't go in there!

Presley squealed, and Tom winced.

They followed the mangled grass and bushes, Tom, all the while, keeping one eye trained on the forest. A flicker in the trees caught his attention. It came from behind a group of fallen branches. It glinted silvery and metallic.

He slipped down the ditch and crept into the ominous forest. Presley followed with heavy panting. Tom's heart bounced in his chest as the legs cranked him forward. The grass licked and grabbed at his legs, trying to pull him down. But it *had* to be there. If not, they would be back to square one.

Don't you get it, Tom? Don't you fucking get it?

The reflection shone again through the trees.

They walked closer.

A snapping sound, together with a chilled wind, made Tom stop. Where had the sound come from? It didn't matter. He was near the finish line. Nothing would stop him now.

They followed the trampled grass, as the fire of determination inside Tom almost burned him up. "Hang in there, buddy," he said. "Not much left. We will make it."

Presley whined.

Under some leaf covered tree branches, the trucks backside exposed the dirty metal handles and the soiled chassis.

Tom's eyes drained of tears and relief filled him.

No! Don't get any closer! It's not what you think it is!

Tom hurried past the backside, moved along the truck's grass-caked wheels, and toward the open door. He stumbled over some broken iron rods. A ripped up roll of toilet paper trailed down the stairs. Whatever had been in there, it had torn up his backpack and pulled out all its contents. The map of Dalton Highway laid in small bits all over the hill, trailing farther into the forest. The food was gone. The water bottle was broken and void of any liquid. Everything was destroyed.

His hope receded like a wave in the ocean, but he still had the truck, the thing he needed most.

He stepped onto the stairs and pulled himself into the cab. Squinting in the darkness of the interior, where crushed glass covered the seats and the floor mixed with more bits of toilet paper. The glass pieces glinted a bit in the now yellow moonlight above. The roof and the seats were covered in frantic scratches, like someone had tried to claw their way out in a state of panic—like that Norwegian man.

Tom swallowed hard.

The place he once had counted as his second home, his rolling workplace, the security it had given him through the years, was now a horror chamber. Blood spatters covered both the door and the steering wheel. There were even a few drops on the floor. But he didn't have time to ponder its origin.

It's over, trucker!

"Soon, it will be over," Tom whispered, went down against the grass, staggered to the tank and unscrewed the fuel cap as fast as his trembling fingers would allow. The fuel cap fell to the ground.

He turned around. Facing the forest again. "Come on!" he shouted. It echoed back to him. "We're here! Come get us!"

Together with Presley, they settled into the cabin, and Tom closed the door.

He pulled out his pack of smokes, looked at the last cigarette, and smiled. He only had one chance to save the world.

CHAPTER

44

THE DARKNESS CAME CLOSER, and the night grew colder.

It didn't come as a surprise when twigs cracked, bushes rattled, and tree branches scratched at the truck. The Devil's laugh busted out, grating at Tom's soul like a motor struggling to start.

Tom tried to tamp down the laugh, but deep inside him, a terrifying force swelled, a reminder the worst hadn't come yet. A fearsome chill ran along his spine, and his vision exploded in a large, white, dizzy vortex, where everything dissolved into a vacant stillness. He sat paralyzed inside the truck, in a dreamlike world, captured by intense subconscious forces, overcome by memories that swept through him like an attack from a captured poltergeist. This was it, the moment he had waited for, the moment where he would save the world, and win back his freedom. Presley sat next to him, panting, his eyes rolling around the cabin. But how good was the plan?

A faint, metallic scratch came from the back of the truck, like claws scratching iron.

Tom tightened his grip on Presley's leash and held his breath.

The dog stopped panting.

Another scratch. This one a bit closer.

Tom's mouth went dry.

Without warning, the glass from the passenger side window exploded. Tom screamed and tried to block the splinters, but it was useless. Bits of glass sparkled over every surface. The Devil crawled his way through the opening like a spider hunting prey. His sharp, bony fingers grabbed at Tom and Presley while he squeezed out a putrid groan.

Presley barked, and Tom flung himself backward, trembling for the door handle. He squeezed it, and the door fell open. He kicked the Devil in the face and fell backwards through the open door. He tumbled to the ground below, taking Presley with him. The slam against the slippery but soft ground knocked away his breath. For a couple of seconds, his lungs tightened in suffocation. His sight blurred, and his hearing faded.

The world came back to him again when Presley's bark grew higher. The dog was next to him, barking at the cabin.

Tom lifted his head. The truck's door stood open, and the Devil was still in there. Despite Tom's agony, he shot up from the ground and slammed the door closed.

A stifled growl erupted in the cabin.

Tom jumped back and sucked in a breath.

Dark, to the limit to black, blood flowed out of the door seam in two thick rivulets. On the truck's steps lay two bony fingers still crooked in a wicked grasp. In the window above, the Devil's face appeared. When Tom's eyes met the hellish portals to the Devil's soul, it was like the world stopped. The Devil's look of shock morphed into a menacing grin, his eyes darkened into hatred, and his lips pulled up in a tight line filled with monstrous rage.

They now faced each other closer than ever. And it was just that thin glass between them both.

Tom stiffened, but this was his only chance. He pulled the mangled cigarette package from his chest pocket, tore out the last cigarette with his mouth, and lit it on fire with shaking hands.

He hurried away to the tank, when the windshield shattered into thousands of jagged diamonds. The Devil flew right through the mess. He landed, bare feet on the smashed truck nose, as glass splinters rained down like tiny hailstones. The Devil curved his entire body backward into a distorted fright. His arms and shoulders dangled straight backwards as his head lolled, like his neck had been broken. Dark blood dripped from his truncated fingers. He stared at the treetops and opened his mouth in a shriek that split the night with evil. His shriek grew higher until it vibrated through Tom like an aircraft engine. But even worse, behind the Devil, a shadow grew from his shriek, higher and higher, until it reached the tree tops and covered the whole forest in complete darkness. The shadows of thousands of condemned souls fought each other to reach a way out of the dark and burning hell. The trees and ground shook in waves. Something hid together with the condemned souls inside the Devil's shadow, something alive but dazed by the fiery flames of hell. It struggled to get out of the dark prison, reaching for the infinite light and freedom.

Tom couldn't move.

The Devil turned. "There you *are* dog," he said with a broad smile and glanced at Presley. "Now … I have to *eat* you."

Presley growled and tore himself out of Tom's grip. The cigarette flew out of Tom's hand, bounced against the tank, and rolled under the truck.

"*No,*" Tom hissed, but the dog was already on his way to the Devil. "Presley! *No!*"

Tom's plan was spiraling out of control, and there was nothing he could do.

Presley jumped at the Devil tore at his leg with a fierce growl. He ripped the Devil down off the truck and slammed him against the spongy ground. The Devil waved his arms in the air and bubbled out harsh laughter. He kicked his legs like a desperate, dancing monkey. Presley tore at him back and front, but the Devil kicked and laughed. One of his bare feet hit Presley right over the nose. The dog winced, released his grip, and withdrew.

An emotional arrow hit Tom in his heart and pushed itself deeper into his shoulders. Something, whether it was a spiritual achievement or an overpowering sense of vulnerability, made him grab a broken iron rod from the grass. He staggered toward the Devil. The few steps he took could've been the slowest and most energy-intensive steps of his life, but when he took power of the iron rod, all logic fled his mind. The Devil tried to get up, but Tom pushed the iron rod right through his right eye with a sloppy, hollow pop. The Devil let out a dark, guttural shriek and his body folded. The howl gurgled from deep in his throat.

Presley attacked again. This time he locked his jaws on the Devil's face and shook with his lanky, knotted body. Something inside the Devil cracked. The Devil curved his spine in unnatural desperation while his penetrating, whirling shriek disappeared into the blackened, isolated forest. With desperate jerks, the Devil grabbed at the iron rod protruding from his eye socket. With the fingers Tom had left him, he managed to tear it out. A slick, crunchy sound filled the air, and his eye followed the iron rod, like a suction cup. The colorless glob, with its tangled eyelashes was speared through, and torn, bloody connective tissue dangled from the rod like wayward electrical cords. An odor of dirty copper, raw meat, and rot rushed into the air. Presley continued ripping at the Devil, whose knuckles popped as he tried to rid himself of the crazed animal.

Adrenaline rushed into Tom's body. He needed to get Presley away from there. Needed to fulfill his plan.

The Devil continued to claw and snarled at both Presley and Tom. He got a hold of Presley, slammed the dog against the ground, and pressed his claws into the dog's stomach. Presley whined and twitched with convulsions. Tom couldn't stand it. He kicked at the Devil's head, and managed to rip the dog out of his grip. But before he could fully free Presley, something slammed against his face. The hit forced him to the ground. Air spewed from his lungs, like a deflating balloon. A thick liquid ran from his right eye. He blinked and for a short moment had no idea where he was. Everything joined together in one big blurry performance. Pain bubbled up on the left side of his face. It continued its way to his shoulders and down to his left hip.

The Devil stood in front of him. He stuck out his black forked tongue and tasted the air like a snake. His crooked fingers pierced Tom's flesh, while the one remaining eye stared into him. The Devil's putrid lips once again knocked into a grotesque grin. "You *can't* ...kill *me*." He opened his mouth in a distorted gap and snapped his teeth at the air like a rabid dog. A crackling groan filled Tom's ear. The Devil's teeth clacked together, over and over again. He threw himself at Tom, arms wide like an attacking eagle.

In that moment, he could have killed Tom, if Presley hadn't jumped up one more time and tore the Devil down into the undergrowth.

Tom rolled under the truck, his pulse booming. He reached for the cigarette with shaking fingers. The glowing tip burned his palm. He tightened his grip. He fumbled the cigarette to his lips and inhaled. Had to keep it lit.

A shrill shriek filled his ears. From whom it came from, was unclear.

Tom crawled backwards in a hurry. When he finally did emerge, the Devil was gone. But next to the truck lay Presley.

Tom dropped to his knees by Presley's side. The dog's blank eyes stared into the forest as if he were sleeping but with his eyes open.

A sob caught in Tom's throat. He grabbed the dog in his arms. On Presley's stomach appeared long gash. A warm and sticky mess leaked out. "Presley?"

No-no-no.

Tom rubbed his tear-filled eyes and nudged Presley's fur in between his fingers. He shook the dog hard. "Presley?"

The dog gave off a quiet groan and gasped for his breath.

Tom leaned his body against the truck and shuddered. The cigarette still smoked in his mouth. They needed to get away from there. Presley needed help.

At the same moment, the scuffing sound of bare feet slid across the metallic surface of the truck's roof, together with a harsh hissing.

Tom's eyes widened. He raised his head. Dark, sinister blood trickled from the top of the truck. The Devil was up there. But not for much longer.

Tom lifted Presley onto his injured shoulders with a grimace and staggered along to the fuel cap. After one last inhalation, he then dropped the cigarette into the fuel tank and ran.

45

THE BLINDING EXPLOSION DEMOLISHED the nearby trees to toothpicks and incinerated the bushes. The intense heat shoved Tom into a splintered tree where he nearly lost consciousness. Although he didn't plummet into total blackness, he still lost contact with reality for a second when the shock wave rushed over him. Presley was thrown into the grass nearby, his breath shallow and raspy.

Next came the sound of exploding glass and the buckling of metal. From what was left of the truck, more flames exploded and charred the canopy of trees. Fire swallowed the entire scene.

Tom tried to crawl to Presley, but he couldn't move. His right leg was stuck. He glanced at it, and his vision blurred. A branch had jammed its way through his right calf. His eyes widened, and panic constricted his chest. He dug his fingers into the grass and tried to pull himself toward Presley with all his remaining strength.

The flames crept closer.

The branch caught in the tangled weeds causing a bubbly, wet sound from the mutilated tendons and ligaments. Then with a snap, the twig broke and Tom fell forward, his face slammed against the ground. Blood pulsed out from the sheared, branch-torn muscles.

Tom couldn't ignore the pain. The heat from the explosion scratched against his face with stinging nails, as everything around him stood in a bright red light. The birds had disappeared from the sky, and the whole forest around him crackled with flames.

A faint sound searched its way out of the fire. Tom turned his pulsating head to the blaze, and his vision doubled. There, illuminated by the fiery glow, was the face of the Devil. It hung like molten rubber, while his skin dripped off like melted candle wax. His rotten teeth fused together, while his lips dripped away.

Tom continued to claw his way toward Presley. The raging heat evolved like a thousand steel nails scraping his.

Presley whined and gasped for air.

Tom's blood boiled in his veins.

The thick black smoke of poisoned gas penetrated the tree branches and disappeared into the dark sky.

Tom grabbed at some nearby roots. He tried to drag himself forward, but everything went in slow motion now. His eyes blurred even worse, and his muscles shook. "Go, Presley!" he bawled. "Save yourself! Run! I love you, buddy. I've always loved you. Please, *go*. Now!"

But the dog didn't move. He lay still, his eyes wide, as he continued to gasp for air.

Tom glanced back towards the flames. His worst fear was the Devil would crawl out from the fire to get him, but nature didn't trick him again. This time, Tom had won.

He clambered on toward Presley.

The flames danced with the trees behind him, melting everything in their path. The heat singed his hair and licked at his neck. He couldn't give up now. They were so close. The road wasn't far. Embers floated in the air like fireflies. If he didn't get away from there now, he would burn with the forest, and Presley would too.

Tom used the last of his remaining energy and crawled to Presley. He gripped the dog's bloody fur, sweat pulsed out of him, and his muscles were ready to quit.

Two diffused, round lights emerged through the darkness.

Tom forced himself to stand, with the help of a nearby tree, but he couldn't use his wounded leg. It ran with blood. But he had to get back to the road.

Behind him, a snap and crunch echoed, as one of the trees lost its grip on the ground and fell on the truck's burning roof.

Tom was about to drag away Presley, when another sound caught his attention. It came as a delightful melody, like it had been composed by a musical genius, with the most beautiful undertones he'd ever heard. The melody died as suddenly as it had been born, and the flames continued to pursue him.

Tom hopped on one leg and drug Presley behind him. His nerves were scraped thin with fear and agony. Every cell in his mauled body now screamed. All the noises around him started to fade as if his ears were filled with cotton.

The road was only a few yards away from them.

The two light balls came closer. Behind Tom, a fierce crack broke through the night, and the flames engulfed the forest into a single flame.

He gritted his teeth. He *had* to continue. With almost no feeling left in his body, he pulled himself up the slope, dragging Presley behind him.

The fiery tongue licked after them.

The lights on the road were now in front of them.

Tom's body collapsed, and all sounds faded to darkness.

The world silenced.

CHAPTER

46

TOM'S EYES FLICKED OPEN at the sound of ravens circulated above him. Their presence was invisible in the dark, mottled sky. The slice of their black iridescent feathers through the wind and flames hummed in his ears. They were waiting for him to die, so they could hack him to bits and fill their stomachs.

Tom tried to reach behind him for Presley, who gasped for breath, but his muscles revolted. "I'm sorry," he whispered. "I'm so sorry."

From the road came a humming and a powerful light.

Behind them, the fire continued to devour the forest, and the ravens still circulated hoping for some easy food.

Tom squeezed his eyes shut, as his energy drained away.

47

THREE WEEKS AFTER THE accident, Tom Richards sat on a chair in a room at the Alaska Psychiatric Institute. He was dressed in the institute's signature attire, thin blue pajamas along with slippers. His psychiatrist, Laura Hensley, sat in front of him with a notepad, ready for today's meeting. It was their second session since the enrollment. The first one had not yielded much in the way of results, as Tom didn't give many answers. When Laura pressed the tape recorder this time, it would be different.

She cleared her throat. "Tom," she said. "This is our second meeting together, and I want to start by saying welcome here again. As I mentioned at our previous meeting, my name is Laura Hensley, and I am a psychiatrist here at the Alaska Psychiatric Institute."

Tom sat rigid in his chair, hands squeezed between his knees. His beard was disheveled and his hair too. His eyes were dark and his face hung with fatigue, but he nodded at her welcome.

"To start today's meeting," Laura continued, "I would like to point out that everything that is said here today is confidential. This means that everything being said here in this room today, will stay here."

Tom sat quietly.

Laura continued to talk, "You were in an accident before you came here, which made you end up in the hospital. At the hospital, you talked to a doctor about certain things you had experienced before the crash. I gather that some things in life have been difficult for you, with some distressing experiences. You are here with us to see if our treatments can help you feel any better."

"Help?" Tom whispered, then raised his voice to a normal tone. "I don't need any help."

"You've been here with us for three weeks now, Tom," Laura noted. "What do you remember from the time before the accident?"

"Everything," he replied immediately. "*Almost* everything at least."

"What do you mean when you say 'almost everything'?"

"Some parts of my life have consisted of blackouts."

Laura nodded. "When did these blackouts start?"

Tom winced. "I've had them all the time, ever since I was a kid."

Laura hummed and filled in something on the paper. "Did you have any blackouts in the days before the accident?"

"No," Tom answered with a delay. "Just the…voices."

"What voices do you mean, Tom?"

Tom pointed a shaking finger at his head, like it was a loaded gun. "*Those.*"

Laura wrote on the paper again. "When did you start hearing these voices?"

"Long time ago" Tom replied, shrinking in his chair.

"What do the voices say?"

"The truth," Tom whispered.

"What's the truth?"

Tom pulled his hand through his hair and sighed. "They want me."

"Who, Tom?"

"Those who rule this country!"

"The government?" Laura asked.

Tom didn't answer, but glanced absently down at the floor.

"How did you find out they were after you?"

"When I realized that I couldn't pay all the bills," Tom said. "By then, I realized they would use other methods. At first I just thought they would take the house from us, but it was probably easier to just kill me. Don't you agree? They tried to poison my food and such. But I escaped their attempts. That's when I realized they had sent me along Dalton Highway to do God's work. They wanted me to kill the Devil. They used Presley as a lure. They steered him. And I did what they asked for."

"Who is Presley?"

"My dog." Tom smiled slightly. "He's my everything."

"I imagine it must have been very hard for you to experience this. Have you ever felt the need to protect yourself?"

Tom made a grimace. "I would do anything for them not to hurt me."

"What about the need to hurt or kill yourself?"

Tom shrugged. "The thoughts have been there."

"Do you ever drink alcohol or use drugs?"

Tom didn't answer.

"What if we go back to the voices, Tom? Did they tell you to take the drive along Dalton Highway?"

"I needed the money. I thought it all would end if I just paid those fucking bills. But it was too late. I took the job for Margaret's sake. And Presley's."

"Who is Margaret?"

Tom smiled. "Margaret, my wife, of course. Who else? But, I think they drafted her into this. And her mother, too."

"How many voices do you hear, Tom?"

"It's always been my own, but I haven't been able to control it. But after the crash, it escalated into more."

"Do the voices sound like you hear my voice right now?"

Tom shook his head. "More like inner voices."

"Have there been any changes in the way you think?"

"I don't know," he said. "It's all been a mess lately."

Laura used her pen again. "Do you ever feel like other people know what you are thinking about?"

Tom shook his head again.

"Where do you think these voices come from, Tom?"

"Magnetic field signals," he answered without thinking. "They can control all of us if they want to."

"Can you feel a psychical sensation when that happens?"

"No," Tom said and sighed. "It's just coming."

"How did you come up with that conclusion?"

"The voices told me."

Laura hummed. "How have you been coping with this other voice you mention, for such a long time? Your own, uncontrolling voice?"

"When Margaret's around, it's not really there."

"Margaret seems to have a big impact on your life. When did you meet her?"

"Fifteen years ago."

"Have you told her about that voice experience?"

"What difference would it make?"

Laura took a deep breath, and hesitated for a few seconds. "Could it be that Margaret isn't real?"

Tom gave her a dirty look. "Of course she's real! Do you think I'm a fucking psycho?"

"I think you have some troubles that prevent you from living a normal life."

Tom bared his teeth. "How dare you state she isn't real?"

Laura browsed through the papers she held. "Reports from the hospital show that you have been visited several times by what the doctors call an 'imaginary friend.' When they asked you who was visiting, you told them it was your wife. But nobody has been visiting you, Tom."

"No, no." Tom laughed and put his hands in his face.

The next second, he broke off the laugh and turned his head aside, staring into the corner of the room.

"I can see you're staring away now, Tom," Laura said. "Do you want to tell me what's happening?"

Tom slowly turned his face to her. "They want me to hurt you."

"Are they saying why you should do that?"

"Because you work for those who rule this country," he answered immediately. "And they also tell me you will never let me out of here."

"Do you believe them?"

Tom started to grin. "Should I?"

"In the past, Tom, have you ever had anger issues?"

"Are you scared now, Doctor?" Tom continued with his grisly grin. "You should be, because I will do *anything* to get back my freedom."

What happened next, Tom would, at a later meeting, explain as a blackout. But the reports show that Tom jumped on Laura and tried to rip her throat open with his bare hands. He never succeeded. The security guards bolted in, tackled Tom to the floor, and forced an injection of tranquilizers into his arm.

***

One month after the catastrophic accident between Happy Valley and Sag River Overlook on Dalton Highway, where Tom Richards had crashed, about three hundred acres of forest had been destroyed by the resulting fire. Now, it was nothing more than a dark, dead spot where firewood lay in carbon shards spread out over the burnt soil's surface. Bushes stood naked next to charred trees against the winter sun above. A few pines, most some young Sitka spruces, had, despite all odds, survived the extensive blaze. Some birds and insects searched their way through the devastation for the warmth and scant nutrients nature had created. Plants already had started to grow again and search for the sky. Not far from there, by the 355 Mile Wayside, was a restroom where someone had put up a picture from the newspaper of a German Shepherd dog, named Presley, who had survived the catastrophic crash, despite grave injury.

It would take time for nature to build itself up again and conceal the past horrors.

Lightning Source UK Ltd.
Milton Keynes UK
UKHW010204301221
396364UK00011B/450/J